SWORDS AND SECRETS BOOK 1

THE CORUNDUM
CONUNDRUM

CASSANDRA
LEUTHOLD

The Corundum Conundrum
Copyright © 2018 Cassandra Leuthold
All rights reserved.

Published by Green Hill Press
South Bend, IN

ISBN-10: 1-947367-00-5
ISBN-13: 978-1-947367-00-5

This story is a work of fiction. Names, characters, and events are products of the author's imagination or are used fictitiously. Any resemblance to actual events or persons, living or dead, is coincidental.

Cover design by Deranged Doctor Design

for Gaia, Croft, and Keeler

The Corundum Conundrum

Chapter 1

Walter Grass raised his longsword high in victory. "Wulfgraad, I've retrieved the item I sought to return to you for so long."

In his other hand, Walter extended a swath of blue cotton fabric. The metal piece strung onto it glinted in the late afternoon light.

Wulfgraad held her pale-yellow paws to her face as she squealed in delight. "It seems like ages since I saw it last."

Walter tossed the found object several inches into the air and let it fall back into his palm. "Yup. Three days later, here's Bessie's favorite bell."

Wulfgraad threw her arms around Walter, her soft chin grazing his forehead. "Thank you so much." She gave him a quick, wet lick on the cheek. "Bessie won't go out to pasture unless I tie this around her neck." Wulfgraad barked, and a black-and-white-spotted cow ambled out of the red barn behind her. Wulfgraad made quick work of securing the cornflower-blue fabric around the animal's neck. She swatted the bell with a playful paw, and it clanged.

Bessie the cow wiggled her ears and shifted her legs in a subtle dance.

Wulfgraad set a paw on Walter's shoulder. "I knew I could count on you. Your finding skills are better than my nose these days."

Walter gave a glum nod of his head. "You're welcome."

"What's your ma making for dinner tonight?"

"Turnips and greens, I guess. Maybe a soup."

"That sounds fine. You can get on home. I don't have anything else that needs fixing around the farm today."

Walter flexed his grip on the longsword's handle. "Tell Bessie to be more careful out in the pasture. I might not be able to find her bell collar next time."

Wulfgraad chuckled and covered her mouth with her paw. "As if I could believe that. Go on home. Get some rest for your next adventure."

Walter walked away from Wulfgraad, Bessie, and the barn through the yard. He ran the last few days' activities through his head. Wulfgraad meeting him at the bridge crossing the brook between their families' lands. She wrung her paws together as she described Bessie's distraught nature and what the bell collar looked like. Walter had collected his sword first thing, then moved in a logical zigzag pattern through the pasture. He'd roamed the fence line and combed the tall grasses sticking up around the outside of the stone fence. The iron bell finally glinted at him from beneath the pasture's solitary tree, and Walter snatched it up immediately.

Longsword. Huh. Walter held it up in front of him. It was only his imagination that made it a sword. The elongated stick he wielded had no cross-guard to protect his hand from enemy weapons. It tapered from the width of a gold piece into a narrow, chipped point, far from the valiant blade he created in his mind.

Walter threw the stick off to the side. He brushed his palms against each other. *No true sword would leave bits of bark and dirt granules behind.* He tucked his hands in the pockets of his moss-green leggings.

He watched over his shoulder as Wulfgraad led Bessie by the collar through the wide, open barn doors. Even as old as Walter had grown, certainly out of his childhood years, Wulfgraad still stood several inches taller than him. She belonged to the race of dog-people known as Cantia. Walter could still hear his dad's reminder of how to pronounce the word.

"It's not cant-e-a, son. It's can-sha. Like, can'tcha say it the right way?" His dad had winked at him with a smile and gone back to his leatherworking.

Wulfgraad wore the same kind of simple clothes they all did in Babbling Brook. She layered a marigold vest over her white blouse and long rust skirt. Her brown woolen shoes peeked out from beneath the hem as she disappeared with Bessie into the barn.

Walter swatted dirt off the sleeve of his rough-spun tunic, the same off-white as the sheep who produced its wool. His "adventure" was over. There was no need to wear the soil of his efforts into the house.

Walter reached the perimeter of Wulfgraad's farm and climbed up over the solid stone fence. He wiped off the grey particles sticking to his skin onto his leggings. The brook greeted him with a gentle murmur of unintelligible syllables.

Walter rolled his eyes at himself. *Yeesh. Give it a break, already. It's not talking to you. It's just moving water.* He crossed the low bridge over the brook, officially now in Grass family territory. "Home, sweet home," he muttered.

Their land was a smaller slice than Wulfgraad's and most of their other neighbors'. His parents didn't need more than they had where their work was concerned. His father, Redley, waved to Walter from his leatherworking station against one outer wall of the house. The clucks of the chickens his mother, Marabee, raised welled up in clipped *bucks* from various points of the yard.

Walter ran toward the stone fence hemming in their small world. He vaulted over the stones with only a single hand planted on them to steady himself. He landed on his feet in the yard just as Marabee rounded the corner of the chicken coop.

Walter rubbed stone flecks off his palms in a hurry. His father glanced over with a knowing smile and a reassuring wink.

Marabee pulled her mouth to one side. "Are you jumping the fence again, Walter?"

"No, Mum." He dropped his hands to his sides.

"There's a perfectly good gate three feet to your left."

"I know, Mum. Thank you. I just used it."

Disbelief twinkled in Marabee's ocean-blue eyes, but it was a reflection Walter recognized. She wouldn't consider him in trouble today. "Did you finish your chores?"

"First thing." Daybreak had streaked the infinite sky overhead with salmon pink and lavender purple as he left the house to pull weeds out of the family garden.

Marabee tipped her head over one shoulder. "How about your mission for Wulfgraad?"

"It's a quest, Mom. And I just finished it."

"Good. In time for dinner. I was about to get your sisters to help me."

From the far side of the house, a stampede of feet thundered on the ground. Walter's siblings, all twelve of them, rounded the corner. They blew through the space between Walter and his mother, his curly hair billowing back from the breeze they stirred up. The youngest children raced past him first, followed by the teenagers shaking their fists at them.

"We're going to get you!" Walter's oldest younger brother hollered.

"You're not getting away with this again!" shouted one of Walter's sisters.

Marabee took a few steps toward them. "Less justice, more cooking, please. Girls, into the kitchen to help me."

Walter's sisters groaned and grunted in frustration. His oldest younger sister held up a yellow skirt. "Look what they did!" She shook it in fury, showing two oval patches of brown on it. "The younger ones smeared mud on all of our clothes. It's going to look like we sat in wet paint."

Walter's oldest brother turned around and pointed to the browned seat of his white pants. "Some of us didn't notice until after we got dressed this morning."

Marabee gathered her twelve youngest children with sweeps of her hands. "Very well, then. Boys to the well for washing, girls to the kitchen for food prep."

One of Walter's youngest brothers, a boy of seven, rubbed his eyes as he stumbled toward the well. "Boys can't wash clothes."

"Yes, they can. Especially when they're responsible for how they got dirty." Marabee ushered the children ahead of her, pointing the girls to the house's front door and the boys further on to the well.

Walter stuck his hands in his pockets and moseyed over to his father's workbench. The solid-stone table was almost invisible beneath a large cow hide. Redley measured it with his amber-brown eyes and made a long slice through it with a knife. He swept the trimmed, uneven edge off the table into the grass.

Walter bobbed his head at the hide. "Is that a new one from Wulfgraad?"

"Yeah. She wanted the meat, so I have something to work on."

Walter cast a disappointed eye on his mother as she followed his sisters into the house.

Redley cut another ragged edge off the pelt. "You wanted her to ask you about your mission, didn't you?"

Walter hung his head. "Quest. Yeah."

"She'll come around."

Walter scoffed and kicked at the grass with his tan leather boot.

Redley shifted the hide on his tabletop. "I mean it. She'll change her mind."

With a belly full of hot vegetable stew, Walter sat down at his grandfather's feet. Thin, red hair sprouted in wispy shocks on top of Hovan's head. His small eyes remained bright and energetic in their azure color. He sat still despite the curved rails on the bottom of his rocking chair that would let him sway if he chose to. Hovan's weak shoulders supported a dark-brown shirt laced up over his chest with a leather cord. One gnarled hand idled on his beige pant leg. Although the rest of the family wore boots most of the time, Hovan sported tan leather shoes.

Walter folded his legs and propped his elbow on his knee. He sank his chin into his hand with a heavy sigh.

Hovan nudged Walter's other leg with the tip of his shoe. "Dinner may be over, but something's eating you, boy."

Walter gave a quiet growl of dissatisfaction. "It's the same thing here, all the time."

"You mean the stew? It had more carrots in it than usual."

"It's everything." Walter sat up straighter to look his grandfather in the face. "The food. The house. The family. The quarrels."

"The quests?" Hovan guessed. "Or missions or errands or whatever you call them."

"Yes, quests." Walter spread his hand out from his side. "The whole hamlet, Grandpa. I've been over every inch of it hundreds of times. I'll be twenty soon, and I've never even been outside the hamlet."

Hovan harrumphed. "What do you suppose is waiting for you out in that big world beyond Babbling Brook?"

"That's just it. I don't know. Every time I bring up adventuring and going on bigger quests to Mom, she shoots it down."

Iron pots struck each other at the other end of the long room and rang out like bells. Marabee spoke up in singsong from the same spot. "That's right."

Walter returned his elbow to his knee and his chin to his palm. "I can't catch a break."

Hovan leaned down toward his grandson. His blue eyes sparkled, even in the shadows. "That's just it, son. There is a huge, wide world past the hamlet's borders. Once you catch a break, you better be ready to catch 'em all. Because there's no shortage of things to do and places to go. There's no end to it."

Marabee let out a high-pitched, "Ha!" Stiff broom bristles followed, scraping across the stone floor. "Don't tell him that, Dad. You're torturing the poor kid."

Walter twisted his torso to confront his mother. "Why is it torture? Because you're never going to let me leave? There's always going to be one more chore for me to do here? There's always one more danger you haven't recounted in exaggerated detail to keep me home forever?"

Marabee kept busy sweeping the floor around the dining table. "That's right. We live in the real world, Walt. There are eggs to collect and buckets of water to fetch. There's always another fight waging or a murderous thief or a monster lurking around the next corner."

"But you get to know about them, and I don't."

Marabee shrugged. "I don't know everything." She tapped the broom's bristle tips on the floor and loosened trapped dirt. "I've spent the last twenty years of my life in this hamlet so I could be alive to tell about the things I know."

Walter blew out a breath and turned back to his grandfather.

Marabee walked over and set a hand on Walter's shoulder. "I'm calling the others to wash up for bed. You can stay here a few minutes more and talk with your grandpa." She opened the front door and carried the broom outside.

The door closed, muffling Marabee's calls. "Children! To the well, please. It's time for bed."

Walter interlaced his fingers and splayed his hands at his grandfather. "There's no use."

Hovan's lips arced into a mischievous smile. "I wouldn't be so sure."

"What are you talking about?"

Hovan gazed at the door. "I know it's your mother's blessing you want, boy. But I'll give you mine instead."

Walter cracked a grin and scratched his head. "I appreciate that, Pops. But a blessing isn't a sword. It's not a shield to keep me safe out there."

Hovan regarded his grandson, stroking his wide chin with wrinkled fingers. "What is a sword to you, Walt?"

"A sword." Walter plucked at his bootlaces. "A sword is a sword."

"Even if it has yellow jewels in the handle? I know it's not your favorite color."

Walter's blue-green eyes widened. "What are you saying?"

Hovan cackled and swatted Walter's knee. "I'm talking about a real sword. One I happen to have amongst my possessions."

"And you'd let me borrow it?" Walter glanced at the door and licked his lips.

"Borrow it!" Hovan batted his hand through the air. "You can have it."

Walter found himself shaking his head. "Ma's not gonna like this."

Hovan's eyes glowed. "She doesn't have to know you're going until you're already gone."

Walter rose up off the floor enough to slide one of his feet underneath him. "She'll come after me. She'll find some way to stop me."

Hovan grabbed hold of Walter's knee. "Are you looking for a break to catch, boy? I'm offering you one."

Walter answered in deep nods. "How do I get out? Where's the sword?"

Hovan slapped Walter's knee. "That's the spirit. Now, here's what we'll do. You get ready for bed as usual. Say hearty *good night*'s to your parents, but keep them casual. I'll sneak the sword into the chest at the foot of your bed. Then, when everyone's asleep, including me, you can sneak out."

Hovan leaned back in his chair and rocked it to and fro. "It'll give you hours of a head start. You can write home from time to time if you like, but don't worry about us. We'll be fine, and so will you. Even your mother." Hovan patted the wooden arms of the chair, carved with maple leaves and acorns. "I'll take care of her fears."

☼

Three small, round pieces of citrine shone embedded in the sword's handle. Walter ran his thumb over them before he sheathed the weapon in the leather scabbard tied to his belt. The rest of his siblings rested as still as well water in their beds, the furniture arranged to fit them all into one room while allowing narrow paths for walking. Walter stood without moving, letting the quiet inhales and rippling snores wash over him.

He cast one last glance into his belongings chest. The bottom lay empty except for an extra tunic and a spare pair of bootlaces.

Walter lowered the lid so that it barely made a sound when it closed. A few moonbeams sneaking in through the window shutters provided the only light to guide him through the room's obstacle course of furniture. He tiptoed through the room, between his brothers and sisters wrapped in their blankets.

Walter snuck out the partially open door to the landing at the top of the stairs. Across from him gaped the doors to his parents' and grandfather's rooms. He wished he could say a true goodbye – just in case anything happened to him out on the road. In case, in some inexplicable manner of happenstance or bad luck, a cutpurse did knock him dead with a cudgel. Or a monster leapt out at him from around a bend and rip out his throat. Or–

Walter pulled his collar away from his hot, sweating neck. He would prove Hovan right. Everyone and everything would be fine. Maybe instead of bandits and beasts, Walter would find something more akin to the Grass family picnics held throughout the year. Yes, that was right. Well, okay, not *exactly* the same thing as sitting down on a spread woolen blanket to enjoy bacon, lettuce, and tomato sandwiches. But *like* a picnic. Only off the family property and out there – somewhere – in the rest of the world.

Swallowing his last lump of apprehension, Walter turned away from his elders' bedrooms and scurried down the stairs. He a threw final look at the kitchen, fire pit, and dining table on his left. He memorized the sitting area on his right with his grandfather's rocking chair, the loveseat where his parents still held hands some evenings, and the array of other seats available for their thirteen children.

A tear of gratitude glided down Walter's cheek for his grandfather. Walter grabbed hold of the sword's handle in one hand and dried the tear trail with the other. He strode to the door and swept it open. In a smooth motion, Walter stepped outside and pulled the door shut behind him.

He then slipped and fell sprawled in the mud.

Chapter 2

Walter wiped again at the mud drying on the front of his tunic. He huffed and let it be. In a world as large as Gladfire, surely someone other than his mother would be available to wash it for him.

No. Walter lifted his shoulders up and back. He strutted down the dirt road with a bit more pride. He was an adventurer now. He owned a sword replete with glittering jewels adorning its handle. Walter could wash his clothes himself and continue on his way without putting anyone out.

He walked on, arms swinging at his sides. He almost whistled but stopped himself. Farmer Dahooti's long, stone house loomed in the moonlight forty feet away. Walter hurried along, eager to leave these houses and familiar fields behind.

He broke into a run, holding the sword's scabbard steady against his thigh. Up ahead stood a white stone arch bending eight feet tall over the road. Dark-green moss grew out of the cracks between blocks. Walter approached the arch. He'd never passed under it before. Marabee had never even let him harvest the clumps of moss from its stones.

She'd shooed him away from the soft, fuzzy vegetation. "Leave it alone. You don't need it."

Walter usually pouted, especially when he was much younger. "I need it for mixing potions."

Marabee took his wrist and led him away from the arch. "You have no need for potions, and you don't need to leave the hamlet, either." And she often towed him home.

Walter stepped up within a foot of a dark patch of moss. It looked like a magical, uncommon thing to him, and it wasn't just his imagination. "I do need you," he murmured. "For making potions." He peeled the moss away from the stones and stored it in his pocket.

He moved back into the middle of the road and took a deep breath, peering up at the white arch. "So long, Babbling Brook. Hello, rest of the Song Lands. Hello, maybe, to all of Gladfire."

Walter took a pace forward. He stopped and peeked around him in the dim night. He speared his hand out, grabbed another fistful of damp moss, and took off running beneath the arch.

Exhilaration filled Walter's lungs. He raced down the road between unfamiliar fields of waist-high grass. "Goodbye, Ma and Pa! Farewell, Pops! Best of luck to you, sleeping hamlet! I'm off to bigger and brighter things."

Walter sprinted until a pain seared through his side, slowing him down. He jogged on, eventually winded and satisfied enough to return to a walk. He grinned at the grasses flanking the road. A patch of iridescent-purple coneflowers brought arresting bursts of color to the side of the road, and Walter plucked their petals. Yellow ladybugs with black spots shared their warm, golden glow in a slow pattern of on and off. Walter collected them in his hands as he picked his way through the group's lazy flight path.

Sharp chittering erupted in the grass near Walter's boots. He jumped away, struggling to pull his sword from its scabbard. The sounds broke into a scratchy, screaming growl. Walter tugged his sword free and held it out, his hand shaking.

A badger's white-and-black-striped head emerged from the grass blades. It cantered across the road in front of Walter and disappeared into the opposite field.

Walter let out some breathy laughter at himself and sheathed his sword. "At least it's a real sword. Not a stick!" he called after the badger.

He picked up his easy pace again "And I can practice with the sword." He jerked on its handle, only freeing half the blade. Walter reset the hilt. He yanked the handle up, almost hitting himself in the nose with it.

Walter rested the sword inside the scabbard. "Maybe I should've waited another night and gotten some useful tips from Grandpa."

He strolled on, making up an imminent threat in his mind. Walter changed the angle of the scabbard with one hand and drew the sword out with the other. Awed laughter bubbled out of him.

He glanced around to share his progress, but only insect chirps and owl hoots met his ears.

"It could get lonely out here." Walter put his sword away and drew it once more to make sure the first success wasn't a fluke. Satisfied, he stowed it in its scabbard and left it there. "I could head to a town. Those have more happening than a hamlet, I think."

At a fork in the road, Walter stopped and put his hands on his hips. A signpost pointed out several way points in both directions. The names were lost on Walter.

"Are these towns or cities or bridges or what?" Walter steadied himself with a determined exhale. "This is my adventure, and it doesn't matter where I end up. When I'm ready for a rest, I'll find my way home again. Anything in between is a bonus to my old way of life."

Walter used two fingers to salute the right-hand trail. "Maybe next time, old chap." He sauntered off down the left path.

The moonlight illuminated a wooden food stand thirty feet ahead. Walter rushed over to it. No one manned its counter, but several pieces of food sat out on a woven grass mat. A notice nailed to the stand read, *Pay well and eat well.*

"Thank goodness. I'm starving." Walter drooled over the assortment of breads, fruits, and vegetables before making his choice. He took an ear of roasted corn as big and heavy as his mother's stone rolling pin. Walter dropped two silver coins into the clay bowl on the counter.

He took a big bite of corn, the tang of salt amid the bright freshness making him hum with delight. Walter munched as he walked, tossing the bare cob aside when he'd finished his snack.

A wet snarl snapped from a hill off to Walter's right. He sucked in a shaky breath and brandished his sword. In the silvery light, a dozen short creatures poured out of the hillside. Walter held his sword up, sweat beading on his forehead and streaming into his eyes. He blinked it away and kept his focus on the creatures. "Should I have left more silver for the corn?"

They all snarled now, gibbering and shrieking. Walter's boots felt nailed to the road, unable to move. His heartbeat pounded in his ears, shaking the ground... wait. It wasn't just his heart. An earth-brown horse galloped in a wide circle away from the hill, supporting a cloaked rider. It tore up the path straight at Walter. He managed to unstick his boots and stagger back a few paces out of its way.

The rider leaned backward, jerking the reins in the same direction. The horse neighed and halted, almost in front of Walter.

Walter could only stare up into the completely shadowed interior of the hood covering the rider's head. He tried to stammer a few words.

The rider extended a green-gloved hand down to Walter. "Get up." His order came gruff and coarse.

Walter threw a glance at the creatures. They advanced toward him and the mounted rider. Merely three feet tall, they bared razor-pointed teeth as they hissed and shouted. They pumped a myriad of weapons over their heads. *Small* knives and maces, to be sure, but their flashing red eyes sent Walter's blood racing through his veins.

The rider huffed. "Get up. Now."

Walter clutched his sword handle in both hands. "I am up. I'm standing."

The creatures screeched even louder as they bore down on Walter. Their eyes widened. Another wave of a dozen creatures emerged from the hillside. The horse gave a nervous whinny and backed up a pace.

"Now!" the rider demanded.

The creatures pulled their maces back to swing at Walter. Knives glinted in the moonlight, and fingernails like tiny claws scratched the night. One of them caught his tunic and ripped it.

Walter cried out and relinquished his two-handed sword grip. He grabbed hold of the rider's hand. Walter jumped as the stranger hoisted him into the air. Walter landed on the horse's back behind his rescuer and slid his sword into its scabbard. He snatched hold of the rider's green-black cloak just as the stranger yanked the reins to one side.

The horse darted ahead, and Walter managed to hold on. One of the creature's torches almost singed his leggings, and his skin registered the heat of the dancing flames.

Walter eyed the creatures over his shoulder until he felt sure he'd gotten away. He faced front again. The horse galloped down the road between other hills. Some were long, low, and rolling like those in Babbling Brook. Others stood taller and narrower like the one the creatures spilled out of.

Walter peeked at the dirt path beneath him, streaking by at a dizzying speed. He lifted his gaze to the tops of the grasses and the occasional tree dotting the expansive fields. "Um, excuse me. Do you know where we're going?"

Only the horse's frantic hoof tattoo responded.

Walter swallowed. "Okay. Can you tell me your name?"

A thick harrumph followed, but Walter wasn't sure if it came from his host or the horse.

"Hey, I'm not quite sure what happened back there." Walter tried to catch his breath. "What were those things?"

"Gnomes."

The voice was so textured and rough, Walter wasn't convinced he'd heard the answer correctly. "No?"

"Gnomes."

"Nose?"

The rider growled over his shoulder. "Gnomes."

"Oh, yes. I've heard of those." Walter shrank smaller behind the stranger. "You can let me down now. As long as you tell me where I am so I can get my bearings."

The rider tugged twice on the reins, and the horse slowed to a stop. Walter moved to jump down.

The stranger reached back and clapped his hand over Walter's knee. "Stop. Have you seen anyone around here who doesn't belong?"

Walter shifted his eyes from side to side. "Around where?"

"This general area."

"You mean, the Song Lands?"

"Anywhere between the White Bog and Sky Gouger Mountain."

Walter shrugged. "I don't know where those are."

The rider snorted. "Have you passed through any of the towns or cities recently?"

"Just Babbling Brook. It's where I live."

The rider's head turned one tick toward Walter. "What's that?"

"It's a tiny hamlet back the other way."

"Have you seen anyone new in this hamlet?"

"Not in years. Unless they were born and being raised there."

The rider's hand constricted into a fist. "Get down."

"What?"

"Dismount. Now."

Walter pulled his right leg up and slid off the opposite hip of the horse. "Can you tell me where we are?"

"How long have you been outside your hamlet?"

"A couple of hours."

Moonlight illuminated white-yellow teeth as they appeared in a wry smile. "Good luck, kid." The rider adjusted the lay of his hood over his forehead. His sleeve parted from his glove enough to display a bracelet Walter didn't notice before. The black gauze ribbon was knotted in place. It held a silver charm of a six-pointed star, a hexagon joining the tips and the middle filled in.

"Thanks." Walter drew a breath to say more, but the rider yanked on the reins.

The horse lurched forward and took off at top speed.

"Where am I?" Walter jogged after the horse and rider.

His rescuer crested a rise in the road and sank out of sight.

Walter gave up the chase and kicked at the loose soil scattered across the trail's packed dirt. He looked around for any signposts or buildings, even a gnome-dwelling hill. Nothing noteworthy jumped out at him.

A spray of iridescent coneflowers shimmered in rainbow-tinged purple from the road's edge. Walter picked them and stashed them in his pocket. If he was going to be lost, he might as well make the best of it.

☼

The moon tracked higher and higher in the sky. Walter trekked beneath the pitch-black expanse speckled with a vast array of stars. He checked over his shoulder for any danger, but he remained completely alone. Except for the buzz of insects and the startling squeal of a small animal somewhere in the grass, Walter felt like the last person left in Gladfire.

"What am I doing?" Walter smacked the hilt of his sword. "This isn't even mine. I could turn around now and maybe get home before sunrise."

He took the scabbard in his hands and examined the three round citrine jewels in the sword's handle. "But Granddad trusted this to me. I can't go back yet."

The gnomes' blazing crimson eyes and pointed teeth made Walter shiver. "Maybe I'm not cut out for this. Maybe this is what Mum's been talking about all these years. The monsters and the strange men on horseback."

Walter stuck a finger through the claw hole in his dirt-covered tunic. "This could've been my chest that gnome opened up."

He plucked at his tunic, caked with dried mud from his own front doorstep. "I could've broken my neck with my first step out the door."

Walter kept walking. Then he noticed that his feet kept walking. He held his hands out from his sides, fingers splayed. "Stop! Quit! Cut it out! Turn away from the trolls and the trees with teeth and whatever else is out there. Go home!"

Walter's legs strode on along the unfamiliar path. "It's safe at home. And there are plenty of people to talk to. And Cantia. And other kinds of animal-people. Plus regular animals that cluck and moo."

But the scenes playing in Walter's mind weren't of pleasant, laughing mealtimes at the big dining table with his family. He didn't dwell on hugs from his mother or helping his father stretch out leather for tanning on the stone worktable. His brothers and sisters argued over their portion sizes at every meal, jostling Walter from either side. His grandfather frequently reached the zenith of a particularly rousing story from beyond Babbling Brook, and Marabee interjected to make sure the rest of it was never told.

Walter curled his fingers around the sword's handle as he strolled with a little more assurance. "This is what I'm meant to be doing. What I choose to do. From now on, without question. I'm an adventurer, and adventure is what I shall find. I won't go home without it."

Within an hour, Walter reached the second arch of his journey. This one was wooden and squared off at the top. Cast iron letters spelled out *Hustle Hub*. Walter strutted through the arch, following the curve in the grey-stone street. Shops sat on all sides of him, thatched roofs topping stone walls. Their massive signs out front displayed their wares in name and picture. *Archer's Aim* accompanied a bow and arrow burned into the wooden placard. Other signs contained carved artwork, like the fully-made bed beneath the words *Wanderer's Respite*.

Walter stopped and stared at the bed's likeness. "Adventurer. Wanderer. Close enough."

He ambled through the door into a room the width of two establishments. A few simple benches adorned the entryway. Round, stone-top tables and straight-back chairs packed the other side of the room.

Walter shuffled up to the counter. No one stood behind it, but a small iron bell waited on its surface. Walter eyed it sideways. "I thought I'd gotten away from iron bells." He picked it up anyway and clanked it a few times.

From an open door on the other side of the counter, a Cantia woman scurried toward Walter. Her tan-and-ruddy-brown fur filled out a small, youthful face. Large, dark eyes sparkled above her black, heart-shaped nose. A pink blouse peeked out from under a brown sleeveless dress. "I'm sorry I didn't hear ya come in. I was catching a nap. Do you need a room?"

"I think so. I've never stayed away from home before."

The Cantia flipped a thin book open with her paw. "Where's home?"

"A hamlet."

"Ah, well, yes. Those are tiny, indeed. They make Hustle Hub look like the Crimson Jewel."

Walter's fingers fidgeted along the counter's edge. "What's that?"

"The nearest major city. One of the biggest in all of Gladfire." The Cantia woman drew her paw down the open page of her book. "Yes, we have a nice, tidy room open for you. Just twenty silver."

Walter gulped. "That's almost everything I've got."

The Cantia's paw patted Walter's hand. "There, there. If you've made it this far, you can find a way to put more coins in your pockets. I know you can."

Walter pulled out his silver. "It's easy to say that, but on the way here, I almost..." *Died.* Walter convulsed and straightened himself up. He wasn't going to give that story any more credence than it deserved. He dropped his silver into the Cantia's paws. "You're right. I'll make my way. This is just an investment in my future outside of Babbling Brook."

"That's the spirit. What's your name?"

"Walter Grass."

"I'm Celestine. Nice to meet ya." The Cantia woman scribbled something in her book with a black quill pen and blew on the ink to dry it. "Your room is upstairs. Turn right, and it's the last door on the right." She handed him a heavy iron key.

"Thank you." Walter hurried to the stairs to the right of the counter. He jogged up them into a long corridor stretching in either direction, lined with closed doors. He turned and found his room, unlocking it at once.

Walter pushed the door all the way open even though it squeaked. Before him, his imagination ran wild with what his eyes told him was a simple, barely furnished room. Instead of a narrow bed stuffed with straw, he saw a wide velvet comforter fit for a king. Where a small wooden chest sat to contain extra belongings, Walter created a giant armoire he could stand inside of with countess robes and complete sets of leather armor.

Exhaustion weighed on him from his long walk through most of the night. He locked the door and dragged his weary feet to the bed. He crawled under the cotton-and-burlap covers. His head nestled into a thin, lumpy pillow.

Walter broke into a full, bright grin. "I made it."

Chapter 3

Whistling seemed to be the only way Walter could possibly express his happiness. He made up a tune as he moseyed down the inn's stairs. He waved to the waiting patrons occupying the benches inside the front door and the Cantia innkeeper behind the counter.

She smiled at him with tiny, straight white teeth. "Your room price includes breakfast. Go ahead and sit down."

Walter breathed in frying meat, browning butter, and stinging black pepper. "What's on the menu?"

Celestine barked in a high, husky pitch. From the other half of the building, abrupt, deeper, gruff barks responded.

The innkeeper nodded. "Barker's famous biscuits and three meats."

"That sounds delicious. I'm ravenous." Walter walked over to the nearest table and sat down.

A short Cantia man emerged from a pair of swinging doors. He tossed his head to bounce stray fur out of his eyes. Most of his fur was snow white except for a tan band between his small nose and eyebrows. He carried out a white-clay plate heaped high with sun-yellow scrambled eggs. Just visible beneath them huddled two golden biscuits shimmering with melted butter. Piled beside them were sausage links, patties, and bacon.

The Cantia deposited the plate on the table.

Walter drooled in anticipation. "You must be Barker."

"I am." The Cantia cleared his throat and motioned to the food. "We serve lunch and dinner, too. When you get hungry later, come back in for something more to eat."

Walter's eyes felt the size of twin moons as he stared at the bountiful feast. "Thank you. I will. Your voice reminds me of someone I met yesterday. He's kind of the reason I ended up here when I did. Do you ride horses?"

Barker snorted. "Can't stand 'em."

"My mistake. You know, Hustle Hub is the first town I've stopped in. And Wanderer's Respite is the first place I've been a patron to..."

Barker wandered away through the swinging doors, and Walter trailed off.

Celestine chuckled in gentle barks from the other end of the room. "Don't worry about Barker. That's just his way."

Walter took a deep inhale and started on his breakfast. After so much walking and running the day before – not to mention his run-in with the gnomes and the horseback rider – Walter all but inhaled his meal as well. He munched with contentment, polishing off all but a few bites of plump, juicy scrambled eggs. He stood up to leave the inn. On second thought, Walter popped the last bits of breakfast into his mouth.

He chewed them on his way to the door and swallowed quickly. "Hey, Celestine. If I want to make money and the only craft I know is leatherworking, where should I go?"

The Cantia innkeeper indicated a direction with her paw. "You can't miss it."

Walter put a bounce in his step and swept out of the inn. He made a right turn and passed several shops before he found *Tans for the Armored Man*. Walter walked inside, numerous windows making the room bright and airy.

A man with straight mahogany hair falling to his shoulders knelt at a tanning rack with his back to Walter. The points of his ears poked through the locks of his hair, and Walter stared. This was no human man.

The leather tanner turned his head to look at Walter. Dark-red eyes glowed like garnets in his gaunt, sepia face. "Whatcha need? Some armor? You're not wearing any." He rose up to his full height, which was a few inches shorter than Walter. He jerked his head at Walter's tunic. "Armor would help keep your shirt clean."

Walter stammered. "You're an elf."

The leather tanner's thin, dark eyebrows lowered. "Moss elf. What of it?"

Walter fetched a handful of moist, emerald-green vegetation from his pocket. "You don't look like moss."

The elf strode up to Walter and snatched the moss. The elf placed the clump on the back of his hand. In seconds, his skin changed until Walter couldn't tell the difference between the verdant clod and the elf.

"Satisfied?" The elf tumbled the moss clump into Walter's possession.

"Yes. Thank you." Walter tucked the vegetation into his pocket. "I do need some armor, but I don't have much money. I've helped my father many times with leatherworking. Is it possible for me to assist you in exchange for coin or product?"

The elf nodded. "Name's Hedrik."

"Walter."

"Didn't ask. You just need something to call me in case you need to ask a question. I don't like being called anything but my name."

"What are you going to call me?"

"Anything I like." Hedrik whirled around on his boot heel. "In exchange, depending on how much you help me and how much you annoy me, I'll outfit you in some armor. Deal?"

"Yes."

Hedrik pinned Walter with his gaze. "If it's a deal, then say *deal*. It's the only way it's official."

"Sorry. We don't make agreements quite like this in the hamlet." Walter would've talked on about Babbling Brook and his family and early quests, but he remembered Barker shunning him at breakfast. Not everybody cared about his stories the way he did. "It's a deal."

"Good. I'll get you started on some basic tasks. If you're better than that, I'll let you do some detail work."

Walter put as much effort as he could into every job Hedrik gave him. He sharpened tools, threaded needles, and carried in buckets of water from a well out back.

Hedrik said nothing except, "I have a design that needs to go onto a belt for a customer."

Walter accepted the challenge and dampened the leather with a little water. He placed his tongue between his teeth and settled in to do his best work ever. Perched on a stool at a marble-top table, Walter's borrowed mallet pressed a metal stamp's simple pattern into the belt. One inch at a time, Walter decorated the length of it with dots and angled lines. He swelled with pride in his craftsmanship by the time he finished. Only then did Walter allow himself to smooth the flawless, swirling black-and-white marble. *Dad sure would love to have something like this instead of his old block of stone.*

Past the end of the afternoon, Hedrik interrupted Walter's hand-engraving of a leather vest. "You did well, kid. The sun's itching to come down, and I want to make my deliveries before I close up."

Walter set his tool down and rubbed his aching hands. "Is it coins or armor I've earned today?"

Hedrik cracked a tight, one-sided grin. "I think you know." He gestured to the wall of his shop where two dozen pieces of armor hung from cloth-wrapped metal hooks. "You can take your pick of what I have in stock."

"Really?" Walter leapt off his stool.

"Not a full set, but I'll let you have a chest piece and leg armor. It'll go a long way toward protecting you, wherever you're headed."

Walter placed his hands on his hips and considered the pieces for sale on the wall. "Do you think any of this will fit me?"

"Fit's not your enemy. It's weight and pliability. What's your specialty when it comes to armor? Light or medium?"

Walter's mouth dropped open for several seconds with no sound. "I don't know. I've never worn it before."

Hedrik burst into guffaws and slapped a delicate hand across his thigh. He stopped laughing and sucked in an audible breath. "You're not joking. Well, you certainly have free rein, then, with your choices."

"What's the difference? I mean, what am I looking at here?" Walter scratched his head.

"Do you prefer mobility or protection?" Hedrik moved over to the wall and patted some of the leather cuirasses and greaves.

"Umm..." The wall of armor seemed to spin and wobble in front of Walter.

"Let me ask you this." Hedrik lowered a sturdy, red-brown cuirass off its hook. "When you left your..."

"Hamlet," Walter droned.

"...did you almost get killed on the way to Hustle Hub?"

"Yes."

"Thought so." Hedrik handed Walter the cuirass. "I'm putting you in medium armor. This will cover your torso."

Walter put the cuirass on while Hedrik peered at the pieces on the wall, tapping a fingertip against his pointed chin.

"Ah!" Hedrik unhooked a pair of greaves and gave them to Walter. "Protect your legs, kid. You'll need them to stand and fight... or run. Whatever the situation calls for."

Walter fastened the greaves around his shins over his leggings. "It'll be a lot harder to kill me now."

Hedrik set his hand on Walter's upper arm for a moment. "Are you sure you'll be heading out again so soon? I could use a good apprentice like you."

Walter adjusted the fit of the thick leather cuirass over his chest and back. "I'm sure. I'm an adventurer, you see. I just decided that. If I wanted to do leatherworking professionally, I could've stayed at home and apprenticed with my dad."

"He's taught you well. He should be proud."

"I'll let him know when I get home."

Hedrik jerked a thumb toward the door. "Get out of here. You've helped me enough for one day."

"And you did me a solid. I think this medium armor's gonna work out great."

Walter let himself out of the shop. With a final tweak to the lay of his armor, he set off up the street toward Wanderer's Respite.

He hummed to himself as he opened the inn door and walked in. What he saw dropped his jaw.

Several "people" loitered around the entryway and the counter. Two humans clothed in dark hooded cloaks cast suspicious gazes on Walter. A tall Cantia man with shaggy white-grey fur held his arm around a shorter, slender cat-woman. Her black-and-orange design made her the brightest, most interesting object of attention in that half of the long room. Someone in a crimson cloak sat on one of the benches with their hooded head lowered so far, leaning their forearms on their thighs, Walter couldn't tell anything else about them.

Smells of charred game, roasted vegetables, and sugary treats called Walter toward his original destination, the food-serving half of the inn.

He stopped humming as he almost choked on his own saliva.

Where hours before he had sat and devoured his breakfast in quiet solitude, even more unsavory characters crowded the dining area. His dreamy haze about what his next meal would be like shattered in the face of reality.

Tin tankards clashed and eager throats gulped down foamy beverages. Someone twirled a dagger slowly on its tip on a marred tabletop. Mocking guffaws issued from a back corner. A card game played out in the center of the room. Two women, one a moss elf and the other human, draped their arms over two of the men's shoulders as they gambled.

Tension quivered in Walter's muscles, but he eased toward the dining room.

Familiar, urgent barks grabbed Walter's attention. Barker carried a tray out of the kitchen and handed it off to a full-figured serving woman with large eyes and a bulbous nose. *Not a human,* Walter realized. *What is she?*

Barker waved his paw for Walter to move closer. "Come back for your dinner?"

Walter scoped out the room of dark armor, glinting eyes, and toasting tankards. "Yes. I'm not sure there's an empty space."

A round-bellied Cantia man seated near Barker howled, clutching his tankard against his chest. "There's no music."

Barker grabbed the Cantia customer by his burgundy corduroy coat and tossed him toward the door. "We don't do that here. And I can't have you nursing one cheap beer all night when there's a better paying customer standing around waiting." Barker ushered Walter to the vacated seat.

Walter scraped together the courage to take a few steps toward Barker and the proffered chair.

Barker slapped him on the back. "Welcome to the Gruff and Scruff."

"I thought it was the Wanderer's Respite." Walter glanced around for a sign.

Barker pointed to one with his paw. *Wanderer's Respite Restaurant between the hours of five a.m. and seven p.m. Between sunset and sunrise, enter the Gruff and Scruff Tavern.* A thick black arrow painted on the bottom of the sign pointed downward.

Walter looked down. A one-inch wide plank of wood separated the stone floors of the inn and its restaurant. Er, at this time of day, tavern.

Walter shrank back. "I don't think I should eat in a tavern. My mother certainly wouldn't approve."

Barker shrugged under his greasy brown shirt and splattered off-white apron. "Sit or don't."

The Cantia cook wandered away toward the swinging doors. A whiff of meaty pot pie and wild-plum cake made Walter's stomach rumble and gurgle. He made a quick slide into the open seat. Encased in his new armor, he assured himself he could sit through dinner without suffering mortal harm.

A green-skinned couple sat on Walter's left, both of them wide-shouldered and muscular. They traded looks of a different kind of hunger than Walter's, and he surmised they wouldn't give him too much trouble. Across from him sat another big-bellied Cantia guzzling from a tankard. On Walter's right, two human men made him feel more at home. Their shifty grey eyes and noisy stew slurping made him feel alone again.

The serving woman delivered a few plates of venison steaks and baked potatoes to a table of snickering, hunched rat-men. She made her way to Walter's side. "Ah, a new customer. Welcome. I'm Selenshia."

"Walter."

She lifted her wide, pudgy hand and ruffled Walter's hair. "You humans are so cute."

He raked his fingers through his loose curls in hurried movements, settling everything back into place. "Um, thank you."

"I'm an ogre. Ogress, to be exact. And I'm here to take your order." Selenshia tapped a sharp fingernail against her tray.

"Bring me whatever's good, I guess."

"What brings you to Hustle Hub?"

"Adventure."

She let out a hefty laugh. "You'll find that here, all right."

Walter leaned toward her. "Who are all these people and creatures?"

"Travelers, like you. Some of them I recognize by face, name, or reputation. Most of them, I don't know."

"Who can you point out to me?" Walter sat up a little higher in his chair.

"Forget most of them. You want to know the most impressive one in this room? Perhaps the whole town?" Selenshia bobbed her head toward the front corner of the tavern, directly across from Walter's seat.

He stretched himself upward. "Who is it?"

"You see the small figure eating with his tiny paws there? He's not talking to anybody, minding his own business. He's wearing the shadowy robe."

Walter lifted a few inches out of his chair. "The charcoal-grey cloak? By the window?"

"That's a rat-man. Rodae, as they're called. No, the *shadowy* robe. A nature mage put a special enchantment on it."

Walter peered at the tables' occupants around the Rodae. "It'd be helpful to know what kind of animal-person I'm looking for."

One robe mesmerized Walter. It seemed grey, black, and invisible at the same time. A barely discernible mist swirled around its folds and fabrics in a constant obfuscation. Walter could never be sure where its exact edges lay. From the ends of the sleeves poked diminutive black paws that held a large fried grasshopper for the creature to nibble.

Selenshia chuckled. "I see you've spotted him. You should be in awe."

Walter watched as the creature selected a squirrel leg from his plate and gnawed the meat off the bone. "What is he? Who is he?"

"He's a fox-person. A Vulyon."

"So many names to learn."

"The world will give you an extensive education. I promise you that."

"What makes this particular Vulyon so special?"

Selenshia bent over to speak in Walter's ear. "He only goes by the name the Fox Thief."

"Is he good?"

Selenshia scoffed and stood up straight to her significant height. "Do you think he afforded that enchanted robe by slacking off? He's one of the best thieves in Gladfire. He's almost constantly on the road. He's come through the inn and tavern before."

Walter's stomach bubbled and groaned. He ignored its pangs. "Do you think the Fox Thief would talk to me? I'm just starting out, and it'd be great to meet someone as accomplished as he is."

"I doubt it. He barely wants two words from me or anybody else. You can see he sticks to himself and goes about his business as he pleases."

"But he wouldn't be dangerous to talk to, right? He's just a loner?"

Selenshia warned Walter with her large, dark eyes. "I wouldn't try it unless I had a job to hire him for." She smacked Walter on the back. "Nice armor. I'll fetch you something good and hot from the kitchen." She navigated the maze of chairs, tables, and rowdy patrons to the swinging doors. "Order, Barker!" she hollered as she passed through them.

A slam twenty feet to Walter's right jerked his focus to the door. A cat-woman padded in, her grey-and-black ears sticking up through slits in her oversized brown hood. She threw a distracted look behind her through the open door as a second *thump* resounded. Her lips moved, but Walter couldn't hear what she said.

Ducking through the eight-foot doorway appeared a pale-green head outfitted in a bronze helmet. Walter almost toppled out of his chair. The creature stood up tentatively and gazed around at the patrons staring at him. A reddish-brown tail of feathery fur ringed in white stripes swung from the back of his helmet. His small, sapphire-blue eyes blinked. His deep voice rumbled in humble intonation. "Sorry."

Walter returned his concentration to his table's inhabitants and trying to think up a way to approach the Fox Thief. His fingers drummed on the table in an idle rhythm. The man two seats away pierced him with a menacing glare, and Walter forced his hands still in his lap.

The gamblers erupted in a cacophony. Half of them snarled insults and curses that drained Walter white as a ghost. The other gamblers laughed, gathered up clinking mountains of coins, and wandered out the door into the evening.

A large, thick hand set a plate of food in front of Walter. He peeked up at Selenshia's grinning face.

"Enjoy your meal." Selenshia took a square cloth napkin out of her apron and tucked one corner into Walter's leather armor at the base of his throat. "Yell for me if you need anything."

She ambled away, and Walter's eyes popped at his second bounty of the day. Fragrant steam rose from a pot pie's flaky crust. A perfect cube of wild-plum cake sat beside it, and Walter indulged himself with a bite. Savoring its sweet sponginess made up for breaking his mother's rule of stuff before fluff. Walter picked up one of the roasted potato spears and munched on it.

His muscles relaxed. A shoving match broke out in the corner by the swinging doors. Two creatures transferred a shady-looking packet from one of their robes to the other. As Walter dug into his pot pie, he felt like a true adventurer, despite how few quests he'd carried out. Here he sat in the thick of it. How much closer to an actual adventure could he get without being out on the road? And walking the roads again he soon would be since his last handful of silver coins would be spent on this meal.

Walter finished his entire plate of food and stood up. Selenshia stopped by to collect his payment, and Walter handed off his last bit of money.

He shuffled through the loiterers and revelers, finally gaining sight of the door.

A female sighed not far from Walter. "All we need is one more. But we must choose wisely. Mrow."

Walter paused in his bid for the door. The grey-and-black cat-woman leaned against the wall to his right, just past Celestine's counter.

Her sage-skinned companion towered at her side. "How do we know who to quest with?"

Walter orchestrated an abrupt turn on his heel and approached the strange duo. He tapped his fingertips against each other in front of his chest. "Did I hear you say *quest*? I'm interested. What are the specifics?"

The cat-woman stood slightly taller than Walter. She regarded him with patient, golden-yellow eyes. "It's a delicate matter."

"Oh, you mean, like a personal thing?"

"An important errand for an old friend. We have a delivery to make."

"What do you need in your party?"

The cat-woman bristled. "Mrow. Pardon?"

"What are you missing?" Walter poked his index finger into his opposite palm. "I may have been raised in a hamlet, and even I know you need a good balance of strengths to get anything good done with a questing party." Walter indicated the ten-foot-tall creature beside the cat-woman. "He's the tank, obviously."

The cat-woman raised her brow. "Hrmmm?"

"You know, the muscle. The force. The offense." Walter knocked on the creature's gigantic bronze breastplate. "With plenty of much-needed protection, I might add."

"Rmm." The cat-woman folded her arms over her shapeless brown robe.

"And what are you? What do you bring to the table?" Walter examined the cat-woman. "Mage? Thief? Scout?"

"Mage. Mrow."

"Perfect! Because I'm a Jack of all trades, so I'll round out the party's skills nicely." Walter landed his hands on his hips.

The cat-woman shook her head. "You're not properly outfitted."

Walter glided a hand down his smooth leather cuirass. "I'm better prepared than I was this morning."

The cat-woman's flashing eyes zeroed in on Walter's head and arms. "No gauntlets. No helmet. Hmm?"

Walter looked up. The green creature offered a kindly, sheepish smile. He pointed a massive finger at his bronze helmet and armguards.

Walter crossed his arms, mirroring the cat-woman. "Where is it you're going, exactly?"

"Into the heart of the Crimson Jewel."

"That's a city, right? That doesn't sound so hard or dangerous."

The cat-woman shrugged. "It could be, especially on the way there."

"Oh, right." Walter tapped his foot. "What if I have secret, insider information that could greatly help our cause?"

The cat-woman purred. "I'm listening."

"I happen to know the famous Fox Thief is sitting in that corner behind me."

The cat-woman's eyes widened. "Most impressive reputation. Do you know him personally?"

Walter sidestepped the question. "I've heard he's open to job offers and won't stand for chit-chat."

The cat-woman tipped her furry head to one side. "You clinch the Fox Thief for our party, and I'll let you tag along."

Walter pumped his elbow down at his side. "Yes! I'll win him over. You'll see. And I'll be a full party member, too. Not some tagalong. I'm gonna contribute." He cracked his knuckles and headed for the Fox Thief's table. "I better come up with something good."

As he drew up next to the child-sized form in the shadowy robe, the Fox Thief polished off a three-inch-long beetle with shimmering purple-black wings. The Fox Thief stuck his tongue out to lick his paw clean but suddenly leapt to his feet on the chair seat. He flipped forward into the air and landed on the table, facing Walter in a defensive stance.

Walter held his palms up toward the Fox Thief. "Whoa! I come in peace. I mean you no harm, okay?"

The Fox Thief remained still and silent.

"It's an honor to meet you, sir." Walter extended his hand. When the master thief didn't shake it, Walter began to worry the animal-man might bite him. He withdrew his hand and tucked it behind his back. "Nobody told me you were mute."

The Fox Thief reached under his swirling robe and counted out a pawful of silver coins. He dropped them next to his empty plate and hopped down onto his chair.

"Oh, I bet it's because I haven't said the magic words yet." Walter rubbed his palm against the back of his neck. "See the grey cat and the green dude against the far wall there? They're with me, and we want to hire you for a job."

The Fox Thief propped his paw on the chair back to dismount from his perch when he froze. He peeled his hood down in a slow, deliberate motion. His short fur was mostly red except for pure-white cheeks, snout, and chin. His fur grew longer on the top of his head, which lay combed back and curled around the backs of his ears. His pale-amber eyes shone with intelligence and curiosity. "Speak."

The single word shocked Walter so much, he wobbled on his feet. "Yes. Right. Sorry. Well, we have an important delivery to make to the–" Walter's memory failed him, and he circled a hand uselessly. "To the big city. So, we don't have any time to waste."

The Fox Thief shook his head and swooped his hood up over his ears.

"Hey, we really need you."

The thief dropped down and landed on his feet on the stone floor. "If you don't know where you're going, I can't help you."

"To the... thing. The place. The jewel-y city."

The Fox Thief turned partway and fixed Walter with his steady gaze. "The Crimson Jewel?"

Walter sighed with relief. "That's the one."

The thief chuckled. "You don't need me. You need a basic map of Gladfire to study."

"I know I'm not good with the names yet, all right? But I know you call yourself the Fox Thief, and you're probably the best thief in the world. Am I getting warmer?"

The thief waited.

"How about this? Is there any way I can earn your trust for just a couple of days? Or however long it takes to make this delivery? I really need this experience. I'm just starting out, and I need to prove myself. Please. Even you started somewhere."

The Fox Thief folded his paws in front of him. "You have two minutes to impress me."

"Shoot. Okay. Um." Walter slapped a hand flat on the table. "I bet I can beat you at thumb wrestling. Is that good? Is that fair?"

The rest of the table's patrons scooted their chairs back and got up in a flurry. They hung back a pace, watching. The Fox Thief climbed up onto his seat, and Walter sat down beside him. Out of the corner of Walter's vision, the cat-woman and her sage-green friend inched closer for a better look.

Walter wrapped his hand around the Fox Thief's paw. "I don't think this is going to be fair to you. You're so much smaller than me, and you don't even have a proper thumb."

The Fox Thief's free paw whipped his hood down from his head. "Count, human."

"Okay." Walter blew a breath out between narrowed lips to focus himself. "Three, two, one. Thumb war!"

Walter's thumb dove down the side of the Fox Thief's paw, but the thief moved his wrist in a sharp motion. Walter countered, spiking his thumb upward and hooking it around. The thief dodged, and a second later, Walter felt a rough paw pad pinned against his skin. Walter stared at it.

"It's called a dewclaw, human. It's as much of a thumb as I've ever needed. I hope you have a better trick up your soiled sleeves, for your sake." The Fox Thief twitched his nose, shifting his cat-like whiskers.

Walter reset his hand around the Fox Thief's paw. "You know what? I'm better at arm wrestling because I get to use my whole arm. That was just a test of your... sense of humor."

The Fox Thief kept his eyes on Walter. "This is a test for you. Count again."

They set their elbows on the table.

Walter licked his dry lips. "Three, two, one. Go!"

Walter sent a surge of might and energy through his arm. He yelled out in triumph and effort, swinging his hand down toward the table. The Fox Thief, keeping his elbow planted, jumped to his feet on his chair.

Surprised and a little alarmed, Walter stopped his arm's momentum. "What the–?"

The Fox Thief kicked his legs out to his right. He spun through the air above his seat, balancing on his elbow. He overturned Walter's near-victory, forcing the back of Walter's hand to meet the table before his own elbow lifted off its surface. The Fox Thief completed his somersault by landing on the table to raucous, deafening applause.

Walter nodded, accepting his bad luck and rifling his hair. "Yeah. Of course you beat me."

When the clapping subsided, the Fox Thief hopped onto his chair and down to the floor. "I believe you've wasted your two minutes."

Walter bent his arm up and made a fist. He patted his modest bicep. "You didn't best me in strength."

The Fox Thief's pale-amber eyes glimmered. "I outsmarted you with the skills I know best. That's the crux of any challenge." He examined Walter from head to toe and walked away, donning his hood as he left the inn.

The table's previous occupants reclaimed their seats.

The cat-woman stepped up to Walter's side. "No Fox Thief, I take it. Mrow?"

"No." Walter stood up and tucked his chair in.

Just as fast, someone storming past him nabbed the chair and drew it up to another table.

Walter ambled toward the mighty green creature waiting by the front door. The cat-woman followed him.

The door opened, and an elf shot inside the inn. She grabbed all of Walter's attention before he could babble his way through a new possibly doomed plan.

Dark, plum-purple hair cut in a severe bob framed the elven woman's face. Her white-grey skin contrasted it. Seven black spots lined the upper curves of each eyebrow, getting smaller until the last dots rested just above the outer corner of each eye. Her irises blared lime green as they inspected the room. Her mahogany leather armor covered a lithe, athletic frame. She held up a paper notice, the top of it torn. "Who posted these?"

Walter was too transfixed by the petite explosion of an elf to bother reading what she gripped in her hand.

The cat-woman lifted a paw. "I did. Mrow."

The elf strode over. "Can you pay better than one hundred silver like it says on the sheets?"

"No. But transportation to the Crimson Jewel is paid for."

"Then I'm in." The elf wadded up the notice and tossed it over her shoulder onto the floor. She propped her hands on her hips. "I'm

Kylani. Looks like we've got muscle and magic and..." She perused Walter's getup and cocked an eyebrow. "Whatever he is already."

Walter scrunched his eyes up a little and looked her over again. Her leather cuirass featured some particularly fine details embossed into its borders, and he had to admit to himself they impressed him.

The cat-woman purred. "My name is Tivara. My traveling companion is Gruhnt. Our new associate remains a mystery."

Walter's eyebrows flew sky high. "I can come?"

"You may have failed to procure the thief, but I trust Kylani's talents will balance out your inexperience."

The elf nodded.

Walter grinned and introduced himself. "Walter." He stuck his hand out to Kylani. She observed it with a twist of her lips like he'd offered her a two-week old fish. He dropped his hand to his side. "Nice armor. You're not a moss elf, are you?"

Kylani's upper lip curved high in disgust. "Hardly."

Tivara sighed and tapped her foot. "She's a sky elf. I'm Fee'li. Gruhnt's half orc, half ogre, and you're human. May we depart now for Robin's Egg?"

Walter held up two fingers. "Two quick questions. That's *fee-lie*? Like *feline* without the N?"

Tivara narrowed her golden eyes slightly with impatience.

"Good. I got that right. And second, why are we going to Robin's Egg? What happened to the Scarlet Gem?"

Kylani smacked her palm against her forehead. "I'd like to suffer only fifty-silver worth of trouble on a one-hundred silver job."

Tivara shifted her shoulders in her robe. "It's the Crimson Jewel, Walter. Reaching Robin's Egg on foot and taking a roc to our final destination is the most efficient route."

Walter ducked his head. "Right. Got it."

A deep, husky, slithering voice resounded behind Kylani. "Got room for another member in your party?"

Kylani whirled away from the voice, sliding herself into the space between Tivara and Gruhnt. Kylani's eyes bulged, and her chest rose in hurried, shallow breaths.

The newcomer raised his palms for all to see. "Jumpy? I apologize. I merely wanted to offer my services."

He lowered the hood of his claret-red cloak in tightly measured increments until it rested on his shoulders. He stood before them, a few inches taller than an average human man like Walter. But their newcomer could never be mistaken for human. Yellow-green scales covered his bald head and neck, the only exposed skin Walter could see. His honey-hued eyes did little to soften his appearance above his short, lizard's snout. Small, horn-shaped scales formed a curved line around the back of the top of his head. They continued down behind his ear holes and formed an intimidating beard under his chin. His medium-heavy build hulked under his thick leather armor, which was a few shades darker than his eyes. When he folded his hands in front of him, his glossy tan claws reflected the inn's firelight. "Name's Slithe."

Walter zeroed in on the lizard-man's timbre. "You sound like somebody who rescued me on the road. Were you riding a brown horse to Hustle Hub yesterday?" Walter rubbed his fingers around his wrist. "Wearing a bracelet with a charm on it?"

Slithe flashed a one-sided grin. "Sorry. I just walked into town this afternoon."

Walter sighed. He'd never find out who saved him at this rate.

Tivara cleared her throat. "Hrxsh. We already have four creatures headed out on a simple mission."

Walter muttered under his breath. "Quest."

Slithe splayed his fingers apart. "I have the thieving skills you were looking for, plus fighting prowess. It takes nothing away from you to let me assist you."

"Actually, it could." Walter met the lizard-man's eyes. "If we get attacked by something, you could kill it instead of me. I'd lose out on the experience."

Slithe bowed over one arm. "My apologies again. I promise not to rob you of what's rightfully yours." His gaze slid sidelong to the Gruff and Scruff end of the room. "You're lucky, you know, that your plan fell through."

"Which one?"

"To acquire the skills and companionship of the Fox Thief. His real reputation is much worse, much darker than his common one."

Walter's throat dried up and closed in a little. "How bad is it?"

"Bloody. Filled with betrayal and the stuff of nightmares." Slithe raised a brow. "Why do you think he's always wearing that magic cloak? If it weren't for that, the duke's guards would've grabbed him years ago."

Walter avoided Tivara's gaze. "Yeah. I guess we got lucky, then."

Tivara took a step toward Slithe and the door behind him. "Very well. You have useful knowledge. We'll take you with us to the Crimson Jewel."

Kylani jumped back. "No!"

Walter stared at her. "Come on. Really? We finally got our party together. Now you want to back out?"

Kylani's bugging eyes pierced Slithe. "You don't need me. What does it matter?"

"You sounded like you needed the money."

Kylani sidled behind Tivara, closer to Walter and the exit. "You sound desperate for the experience."

Walter touched her arm. "Look, I get it. It's a scary world, and anything could happen to us on the way to the Big Red Crystal. We're all freaked out by one creature or another, like this..." He gestured to Slithe.

"Repter," Tivara provided.

"Right. Exactly." Walter rubbed Kylani's arm to reassure her. "We'll be safer with five of us. You get your coinage, and I get to live to put my experience to good use. What do you say?"

Kylani swallowed hard, her eyes pinned on Slithe. She nodded. "I'll come."

"It's okay. I'm learning, too." Walter bucked his chin up at Tivara. "Are we ready to shove off?"

Tivara balked. "Not so fast. We need to gear up. Even short, straightforward journeys can pose their challenges. Didn't you prepare yourself before leaving home?"

"Yes, but I'm out of money now." Walter beat out a rhythm with his flat hands against the sides of his thighs. "Kinda hard to prep without that."

"Join us in the shops anyway. You might learn something important."

Tivara strolled past Slithe and opened the inn door. Gruhnt motioned the others ahead of him. Slithe walked outside, and Walter followed him. Kylani moved close on his heels, and Gruhnt closed the door behind them all with a slam.

Walter jumped.

Gruhnt's mouth squirmed. "Sorry."

Kylani spoke up at once. "Where's the fletcher?" She held up a short bow.

Tivara pointed with her paw. "Archer's Aim. That way on the right. We'll meet back here in front of the inn in case we get separated."

Kylani whisked off, and Walter shadowed the others as they wandered deeper into the commercial district. Slithe lumbered off to a small shop with two thin tools and a keyhole emblazoned on its sign beneath the name *Pick Your Friends.*

Walter caught up to Tivara's side. "What is that place?"

"They cater to thieves, rogues, and pickpockets, I assume."

"Those are lockpicks on the sign?"

"I believe so. I studied at a mage school, not a den of inequity."

Walter's excitement spiked, and he bounded a step forward. "That's right. I've been meaning to ask you about your magic."

Tivara eyed him sidelong. "Perhaps at a better time."

Walter's shoulders slumped. "I understand." He glanced around for Kylani and Slithe. "Do you think we'll ever see those two again?"

Tivara yawned. "They'll show up if they want to get paid, which I assure you, they do."

"Even Kylani? She almost jumped out of her skin when we took on Slithe."

"It's no great matter. One thing I can teach you now, Walter, is that you can only choose your traveling companions to a certain extent. They all carry with them some sort of baggage or other, but as long as you can mostly focus on the task at hand—"

"The quest."

"—everything works out well enough. Here we are."

Tivara and Gruhnt turned off the street at the sign for Heavy Metal Armorers and Sons. The blackened, engraved picture showed a massive hammer above an anvil.

"When are we shopping for Gruhnt?" Walter joked.

Tivara groaned.

The door stood twelve feet tall and six feet wide. Gruhnt opened it and waved his companions inside.

Walter whispered to Tivara as they stepped into the shop. "Is he always this polite? It's freaking me out."

"He was raised with manners, yes. Hrmmm?" Tivara gave him a knowing, prompting look.

Walter whistled a trilling tune and moseyed off to busy himself. Unlike Tans for the Armored Man, no leather appeared on these massive walls. Every piece hung high and low shone, dazzled, and glinted.

Behind Walter, a greeting erupted from the shop owner at the counter. "Gruhnt, my good man! Great to see you."

Gruhnt hummed. "Likewise."

Walter considered the different materials shaped before him, only familiar with some of them. He knocked on an iron cuirass, making his knuckles smart while the armor rang out like a bell. He shook his hand out and resolved to keep it to himself in the future.

The shop owner crowed again. "What can I get for you today?"

A loud thump accompanied Gruhnt's reply. "I'd like to upgrade my shield."

Walter glanced over. An iron shield bigger than a trashcan lid balanced on the stone counter.

The human shop owner hefted it up in his meaty hands. His bulging biceps sprouted veins beneath his rolled-up shirtsleeves. "What kind were you looking for?" He waggled his bushy black eyebrows. "I have rhodium. Just in."

Gruhnt turned his face away, blushing pink across the small apples of his cheeks. "I can't afford that yet."

"One day, you will. And I'll be the one to sell it to you." The shop owner tucked the iron shield behind the counter. He held out a steady fist, and Gruhnt bumped it with his own. "There's a lad. What were you really shopping for?"

"Bronze. Like the armor you sold me."

"We're making progress. Let me know when you're ready to replace that iron mace you're still lugging around."

Tivara arrived at Walter's side and cast observant eyes over the selection of armor pieces.

Walter scrunched his face up. He held his breath and tried not to writhe in place.

Tivara blew out a breath. "You have questions. I know. Ask them."

Walter bounced in place. "Okay. Some of these metals, I recognize." He pointed them out on the wall. "Gold. Silver. Iron. Bronze. But what are these other ones?"

The shop owner called out from across the room. "That top row, that's rhodium. The most expensive metal in Gladfire."

Each piece in the full set glimmered metallic grey like silver, but every curve, dip, and edge held the blackest shadows Walter had ever seen. The contrast marking every inch of it inspired awe in him. "That's beautiful."

Tivara motioned to the set. "That's Gruhnt's ideal armor."

Walter gave Gruhnt a thumbs-up. "You got great taste, buddy."

Gruhnt beamed. "Thank you, Walter."

Another cuirass mystified Walter. He wasn't convinced it was made of metal at all. Even though it was solid, the red-tinged tans and browns that colored it remained slightly translucent. Walter squinted closer. Flecks of ruby, sapphire, and brilliant yellow floated, trapped, within the material. Walter brushed his fingertips against it. "What is this?"

Tivara moved forward to inspect it. "Corundum."

"Where does it come from?"

"Miners dig it up, same as the metals."

"So it's not a metal?"

"No, but because of its resilience, it's just as popular. You never heard of it?"

Walter shook his head and tucked his hands in his pockets. "Babbling Brook is a simple place. At the edge of the Song Lands like we are, we're not exactly a major stop on anybody's trade route. And we do just fine with iron most of the time, thank you very much."

Tivara's mouth curved in a small smile.

Walter reeled backward, clutching his chest. "Did I make you smile? That's incredible!"

Tivara pressed her thin lips into a tight line. "Don't get used to it. Mrow, human?"

"Noted, but about corundum. It must be pretty expensive, right? If it's that popular."

"It's worth more than iron and bronze. Plus the copper and tin used to make bronze. But that's about it."

Walter grinned. "Tivara, I think you missed your calling as a blacksmith."

Tivara paused for a beat. "Walter, this is common knowledge from trading in the world. And traveling with Gruhnt. It has nothing to do with any latent talents."

Walter sucked in a big breath, but words failed him. "Okay. Gruhnt, how's it coming?"

The skyscraping ogre-orc lifted a vast bronze shield that flared out from a flat top and tapered to a definitive point at the bottom. Decorative grooves lined its edges, and a circular sun symbol with wavy lines around it filled its inner surface. Gruhnt held it up next to his cuirass of the same metal.

Walter offered him a casual salute. "It looks great."

Gruhnt squinched his bold-blue eyes into slits and bared his long teeth. He raised his shoulders and drew his sizable iron mace. Its bulk covered in numerous sharp points made Walter flinch. Gruhnt roared from deep in his huge chest, blowing Walter's hair and Tivara's fur back. The cuirasses and smaller pieces of armor rattled on the wall behind them.

Walter quavered and almost fell to his rattling knees.

The corners of Tivara's mouth perked up. "Very nice, Gruhnt. Quite terrifying."

Gruhnt blinked his eyes fully open and entertained a gentle smile. He tucked his mace away behind his back and hung his shield off the back of his cuirass. He shook hands heartily with the shop owner. "Thanks. We'll be back soon."

Gruhnt hurried for the door, opened it, and dashed out into the dark evening.

Tivara followed him at a slower pace. "Sometimes his new purchases make him excited."

Walter stayed close to Tivara as they left the armorers' establishment. "Where to now? Where do you shop?"

"I want potions in case I need to refill my magic during an encounter."

Gruhnt lurked in the middle of the road, growling at passersby with a goofy expression lighting his features. The figures scattered and rushed past him.

Tivara clapped her paws together. "Come, Gruhnt."

The ogre-orc's pounding footsteps resounded behind Walter, confirming that Gruhnt obeyed.

Walter flashed back to the gnomes' crimson eyes burning with fury and hostile intent. "By *encounter*, you mean skirmish. Fight. Battle."

"Precisely. And by acquiring the potions I need, I mean to secure our chances of surviving."

Tivara led Walter and Gruhnt down the path to a round, grey-stone building. Hunter-green moss clung to the earthen patches between the rocks, and Walter reached for some.

Tivara shook her head. "Consider that private property, hrow."

Walter shrank, feeling sheepish. "Sorry."

"There will be plenty of ingredients to harvest on the road." Tivara pried the shop's door open.

Walter brightened. "Oh, and I will nab them. I'm pretty good at that, finding things to save for later."

He trailed Tivara into the shop. The sales counter formed a ring in the center of the room. Five continuous shelves lined the outer wall, packed with bottles in various colors and shapes. Some of them had tall skinny necks, and others had large, round bodies.

The saleswoman in the middle of the counter space waved them in. "Welcome to Lottles of Bottles. Welcome back, dear mage. I made up new batches of health and magic potions this morning."

Tivara set her paw on Walter's arm. "You know which color is which, don't you?"

Walter's muscles relaxed, and he rocked his weight onto one foot. "I do, actually. Thanks to running around the hamlet collecting bug parts and different plants. I've mixed a few potions behind the chicken coop when my mom wasn't looking."

Walter sauntered over to a section of shelves and flourished his hand at the bottles. "The green ones are for health, and purple is for magic."

Tivara poked her paw at the colorful assortment. "Which one's vitality, mrow?"

"Red." Walter pulled a cylindrical, apple-red bottle off its shelf. "Restores stamina and constitution. It came in handy on some of the farms. I've seen bottles like this before."

The shopkeeper gave a knowing giggle. "On a farm? Not like that one you're holding. That costs three hundred gold."

"Putting it back now. Carefully." Walter eased the bottle onto its empty place on the shelf. "Tivara, it's all you." He bowed and gestured to the counter.

Tivara conversed in low volumes with the shopkeeper. Walter folded his arms behind his lower back and perused the array of bottles he didn't recognize. Several sparkled iridescent purple like the coneflowers he'd picked on the way to Hustle Hub. A few bottles carried contents that swirled in perpetual motion. Other bottles seemed to contain shifting mist within their glass exteriors. An entire section displayed brown bottles, knitting Walter's eyebrows together.

Tivara paid for a few potions.

Walter called over to the shopkeeper. "Excuse me. What are these plain ones for?"

"Each mixture raises a different skill for about a half hour. If you want a concoction that'll raise your skill for longer than that, I have those in a secret stash."

Walter couldn't begin to guess what a potion like that would cost him. "I'm just browsing."

Tivara stalked toward the door, and Walter swooned with relief at leaving the shop. He held the door open for Tivara and returned to her side for the walk back to the inn. Gruhnt fell into step behind them.

Walter glanced high over his shoulder at Gruhnt. "I see why you didn't want to go in there, big guy If I broke one bottle in there, I'd be working for a month to pay it off."

Tivara spoke up. "And the door's too small."

"What?"

"How do you fit a ten-foot creature through a seven-foot door? At least the clearance at the inn is taller."

"Why do different shops have such varying entrances?"

Tivara jerked toward Walter to dodge a man carrying a wide basket of potatoes. "Stereotypes, in a word. Most of the larger races like ogres, orcs, and magma elves tend to specialize in fighting skills. Magic and trickery are more common amongst the average and smaller-statured creatures."

"That makes sense. When your biceps are as big as domed roofs, why not take advantage of them?"

"There are advantages in hidden strengths as well, mrow. You might do well to remember that."

Walter spied up ahead through the sparse evening crowd. Slithe lingered by the inn's door like an unmovable sentry. Kylani waited eight feet away from him, her glassy eyes skittering from him to the passersby.

Walter could hardly believe his eyes. "Tivara, is your night vision better than mine? I swear, our whole party's here at last."

Tivara made a rumbling hum. "Mrrr. Yes, I see better than you, and yes, we're all here."

The five party members converged into a circle at the side of the road.

Walter's nerves buzzed with excitement. "Are we ready? Which way do we go?"

Tivara raised a paw into their midst, gaining everyone's attention. "Not quite. I have a surprise for Walter."

Walter blinked hard. "I didn't know I could fit this many surprises into a day."

Tivara lit up with the hint of a smile. She reached into her satchel and pulled out a small green potion. "Here, human. Mrrr. A gift. If you can't yet afford your own supplies, perhaps this token may aid you in your travels."

Walter accepted the bottle, his heart fluttering. "Thank you, Tivara. You might've saved my life some day in the future." He slid it into his pocket.

Gruhnt chuckled in slow, deep breaths. "And me. I want to give something to Walter." The ogre-orc produced a pair of iron gauntlets. "I forgot to sell these in Heavy Metal."

Walter held his arms out, and Gruhnt fitted the gauntlets over Walter's hands.

Walter marveled at their sturdiness and the swirl pattern cast into their design. "These are magnificent, Gruhnt. Thank you."

Slithe's voice slithered free. "And from me, Walter. A hunting knife, but it's not as ordinary as it first might seem. It's enchanted – lightly – to imbue its wielder to swing it at twice the normal rate."

Walter's jaw dropped. "That's awesome. Are you sure? I already have my grandfather's sword."

Slithe extended the serrated weapon handle-first toward Walter. "Take it. Magic-infused equipment trumps regular pieces any day."

Walter wrapped his fingers around the hunting knife. White-blue glowing mist surrounded its contours. "What would you do with your original weapon?"

"Sell it."

Walter's heart plummeted. "Just like that?"

Slithe rolled his shoulders back several times in his leather armor. "Staying agile and mobile sometimes means parting with the very pieces that used to make your heart sing."

Walter gulped and slipped the hunting knife through a space in the right-rear part of his belt. "I'll have to think about it."

The others looked at Kylani with an expectant light in their eyes.

The sky elf sighed and rummaged through her pockets. "Here. May it add to your vitality." She plopped a copper ring into Walter's palm. "It's enchanted to give you a little extra vigor when you wear it."

Walter took his gauntlet off and slid the ring onto the middle finger of his right hand. "Any extra skill is better than none at all. I appreciate your support."

Walter fit his gauntlet on again. He swelled his lungs up with a deep breath and let it out into the night. His four companions gazed at him, all of them better experienced and outfitted. His new belongings rested in his pocket, covered his hands, hung from his belt, and encircled his finger. "Hold on," he blurted out. "I'll be right back."

Tearing off down the street, Walter raced straight to Heavy Metal Armorers and Sons. He rushed inside and approached the shop owner at the counter. "Do you buy swords?"

The shop owner propped his strong, hairy hands on his hips. "Not usually, but if you're a friend of Gruhnt's, I'll take something off your hands for a fair price."

Walter brandished his grandfather's sword from its scabbard. He rubbed his thumb over the three round citrine stones embedded in the handle. "Goodbye, my friend. Grandpa put his trust in me with you, and now my new friends have shown their trust in me with their gifts. I know Pops would understand, and selling you can only help me buy whatever else I'll need beyond Hustle Hub. Find a good owner who appreciates you and polishes you right."

The shop owner offered Walter a kind, understanding smile as he took Hovan's sword. "I'll make sure it gets to the right home." He paid Walter in a hefty number of silver coins.

Walter untied the scabbard and set it on the counter.

The shop owner passed a small tin scabbard to Walter. "For your knife. On the house."

"Thank you." Walter hooked the scabbard where his grandfather's sword used to swing from the front-left side of his belt. He sheathed the hunting knife inside.

Walter left the shop and returned to his party. He gripped the knife handle, and their gazes fell on his recent change. "I have enough money now to spend the night at the inn before we head out."

Tivara nodded. "It'll be safer on the road in the morning."

Slithe hissed under his breath. "It's getting late in the evening to find an open bed."

Walter slipped through the gathered group and entered Wanderer's Respite. He sauntered up to the counter and addressed Celestine. "Do you have five beds free for the night?"

The rest of his party stepped into the inn behind him.

Celestine checked her record book. "I have exactly five left."

"We'll take them." Walter settled his bill by setting silver coins on the counter.

One by one, his comrades strolled up and paid for their rooms. Celestine handed out their keys.

Walter turned to the rest of his group, capping his palm over the end of his new knife. "I'm one of you now. All in. First thing in the morning after a hearty Barker breakfast, let's start our adventure."

Chapter 4

The blazing sun rose high and bright in the lake-blue sky. Puffy clouds floated by at a snail's pace, as fluffy as loose wads of sheep's wool.

The party arranged itself in a natural formation as it emerged from the town's main street. Gruhnt walked up ahead with Slithe on his right. Walter and Tivara filled out the middle of the pack with Kylani lagging behind them.

Walter sauntered up the road, basking in pride in his newly acquired possessions. His attention raked the grasses along the pressed-dirt path. He frequently darted over to collect goldenrod with its light fringes of flowers reflecting sunrays off their metallic sheen. He just as often jogged to the opposite edge of the road to pick small rust-colored ants off tall grass stalks.

As he rushed past Tivara to snatch a luminescent ladybug out of the air, the Fee'li mage flinched.

Tivara groaned long and low in her throat. "You told the truth, Walter. Rmmm. You do harvest everything in sight."

"Sorry. Am I being distracting?" Walter encouraged the bugs into his pocket.

Tivara and Kylani replied in unison. "Yes."

Walter brushed his hands clean on his leggings. "Is now a good time to ask questions?"

Tivara adjusted her oversized brown hood over her head. Her ears peeked out through the slits in the top. "Go ahead. If it keeps you from almost trampling me, I welcome it."

Walter clasped his hands together. "Okay. You said you're a mage. But you didn't tell me what school you went to."

"Fire." Tivara's eyes warmed with hunger.

"Really? Is that safe? You're covered in fur."

Tivara held out her paw. Orange flames erupted around it, licking and flitting. Walter squinted at it, inspecting how a miniscule space separated Tivara from her magic. The fiery tongues puffed out.

Tivara's power and control stunned Walter. "What kinds of spells can you do? Like, small bursts or big waves or...?"

Tivara entertained a thin grin of satisfaction. "Bursts. Streams. Shields. I do well for myself, human. Mrow."

Walter flung one hand out in front of him, then the other. "Can you throw multiple bursts of fire at several opponents at the same time?"

"For a while. Then I drink a potion to recharge my store and continue throwing fire."

Walter shook his head in wonder. "I'm with a real mage. But how did you come to choose fire? How do you know it's the best school?"

Tivara's shoulders bunched up. "What?"

Walter laid a hand on his chest. "You can't tell me fire is always the best magic to use in every single situation."

Tivara's right eye twitched. "It does well enough. I've never had a problem bending fire into what I need it to be."

Walter wagged his hand up ahead at a rise beyond a curve in the road. "But if bandits or gnomes ran at us over that hill, you wouldn't be able to slow them down, would you? Isn't that pretty unique to cold magic?"

Tivara bared the tips of her front teeth and held up a paw. "Burning is unique to fire magic, wouldn't you agree?"

Walter eyed the paw with caution, lest it spring into flames. "I'm not trying to upset you. All these facts and choices are why I haven't been able to narrow my skills in any significant way."

Kylani's hand latched onto Walter's shoulder from behind him. Her voice came hard and cold. "You haven't been focusing your efforts?"

Walter started, especially at her piercing lime-green gaze boring into the side of his face. "No. It's too tricky weighing all the possibilities."

"That makes you a liability." Kylani retracted her hand with a rough, miniscule shove and fell a step behind again.

Walter stammered. "No, I'm not. I'm a Jack of all trades, like I said. I know a little about most things. I'm really very helpful. An asset, you might say."

Slithe tossed a comment back from the front of the group. "Everybody starts somewhere."

Walter pointed to Slithe, swinging his eyes between Tivara and Kylani. "That's right. I'm just starting out."

Tivara hummed. "That explains your variety of armor."

Walter peered down at his mix of brown leather and shiny iron. "What? I don't look so bad."

Tivara turned her head away and shook it side to side.

Walter deflated with a huff. "What? If nobody explains it to me, I'm never gonna learn."

Slithe half-turned toward Walter and kept pace at Gruhnt's side. "It's not about fashion, lad. It's about picking a skill in each area and sticking to it. Armor, in this instance. You're cheating your medium armor skill with Gruhnt's old gauntlets. And you're earning minimal heavy armor experience with only your hands clad in metal."

Walter bucked his chin up. "Well, that may be, but they both fall under the fighting umbrella, so it's not the worst idea I've ever had."

Kylani groaned from the rear of the traveling party. "I'd hate to find out what that was."

Walter piped up. "So far, that's turned out to be walking away from my neighbor Wulfgraad's prize bull with a cob of Farmer Dahooti's best sweet corn in my back pocket." He scoffed and rubbed his backside. "You haven't been hit until you've got over two thousand pounds of muscle running at you, peckish for a snack. I'm lucky I avoided the horns."

Tivara chuckled ruefully. Kylani glowered in silence.

Walter splayed his hands. "What now? The impact threw me twenty feet and gave me a bruise the size of an elder-berry pie for two weeks."

Slithe stopped walking, and Walter did, too, rather than come up next to him.

The Repter fighter-thief regarded the human with an icy glint in his eyes. "Twenty feet. I suppose that was horizontal?"

"Y-y-y–" Walter swallowed through a tight throat. "Yes."

"Try falling forty feet onto a stone-and-iron bridge. And missing the stone." Slithe licked his narrow lips. His pink tongue split into a short, white fork at the tip.

Walter shrank back, his breathing eking in with a shallow inhale.

Slithe gestured to Tivara, who'd meandered ahead up a few paces. "I'm sure we all have stories like that who've been out adventuring already. Mage?"

Tivara circled around. "Mrrr? Yes. I was facing six wild cats, and I ran out of magic. I'd drunk all of my potions, and the nearest town was too far away to help me. I resorted to my dagger." She patted the pocket of her robe.

Walter studied Tivara in confusion. "A dagger? What about your claws?"

Tivara held up her paw and flexed it, showing neatly trimmed claws. A sad light hung in the distance of her eyes. "Some of us make sacrifices to live in structured society, human."

Walter's chest expanded inside into a hollow, shadowed cavern.

Slithe clapped him on the back and called out. "Gruhnt? What about you, big fellow?"

The tall, green-skinned ogre-orc paused and turned to face Walter with a wide, goofy grin. "I quite like Walter's gathering of plants. Tivara could mix them into potions that make this journey as easy as sliding a sharpened blade through an enemy's innards."

Slithe tensed his mouth into an appreciative but impatient line. "You're a brilliant strategist, my friend. But the subject's changed."

Gruhnt gave a few solemn nods and let his mirth disappear. "I was keeping watch at the front of the group."

Walter murmured, "Party." He heard a more feminine voice utter it at the exact same time. He glanced back at Kylani, who remained six feet behind him, sulking with steely eyes.

Gruhnt cleared his throat. "What are we talking about now?"

Slithe squeezed Walter's shoulder. "A time you were in some of the greatest danger of your life."

Gruhnt hung his head. "My village caught on fire."

Walter made a move to comfort Gruhnt but stayed with Slithe. Walter had already proven he'd had an easier life than everyone else involved. His pats of reassurance might not mean much. His heart sank into his stomach. "Gosh, I'm sorry, Gruhnt."

The ogre-orc covered his face with his hands. "It was awful. Yurt poles up in flames. Chests of belongings torched. Orcs and ogres getting burned when they tried to stop it. We lost everything. The worst part was I... I..." Gruhnt shook his head in a fit.

The most painful truth of all dawned on Walter like waking up from slumber with the full sun in his eyes. Gruhnt had destroyed his entire village. Walter sucked in a breath and tugged on Slithe's sleeve. "Okay, I get it. Story time's over."

Slithe pulled away from Walter, tossing a glance at Kylani. "There's still one of us who hasn't shared a tale. Sky elf, do you care to join us?"

Kylani pushed her frigid answer out. "No."

"I didn't think so." Slithe strode ahead and caught up with Gruhnt.

Tivara and Walter wandered forward, and Kylani kept her distance behind them.

The group made their way up the path. The weights of guilt and shame dragged Walter's feet along the packed dirt. The rest of them had all lost so much. They'd sacrificed. They'd suffered tremendous hurts and fought against panic to claim their victories and live to fight another day.

What had Walter ever done? Gone sprawling into the mud – on more occasions than he could count. On the day of his run-in with Wulfgraad's bull, he'd promptly given over the cob of sweet corn with a shaking hand. The bull had lumbered away with it and munched on it in the barn's shade. Walter had slunk back onto his family's property, where the explanation of his soiled hair and clothes sent the other fifteen members into hysterics for the better part of an hour.

Walter shuffled along the road, roaming further and further from that humble farmland. *What I wouldn't give for a chance to show all of them I'm more than they think I am.*

A bang of metal against metal broke Walter out of his self-involved stupor. Gruhnt and Slithe had stopped walking. Gruhnt slammed his iron mace against his bronze shield, the same clatter that had arrested Walter's attention. Slithe brandished a silver short sword.

Walter's heart leapt and galloped. "This is really happening." Sweat made his forehead itch as he drew his hunting knife. He looked to Tivara and Kylani for their reactions.

The mage adopted a fighting stance and raised her paws in front of her. Each one erupted into flames, their reflections dancing in her eyes. The sky elf whipped out a short wooden bow and equipped it with an arrow from the quiver on her back. Her lime-green eyes scanned the area with precision.

Walter tightened his grip on the hunting knife's handle. *No, don't do what you* think *you should do. Do what comes naturally, what feels right.* Walter loosened his fingers and reset them. His vision swept the fields around them. "What did you see?"

Slithe tasted the air. "Hear. You must use all your senses to survive."

Gruhnt peered through slitted eyes over the grasses swaying in the breeze. "Something was moving through the grass."

"I don't like the taste of it."

Gruhnt pointed with his mace. "There!"

From the thick vegetation, a four-foot-tall spider sprang through the air. Black-and-white fuzz covered its body and legs like zebra stripes. Bright turquoise mandibles twitched beneath a row of eight glassy eyes.

Walter shivered, and every muscle in his body jerked away from the jumping spider. But his willpower and his bones kept him in place.

More jumping spiders flew out of the field, trailing lines of fine silk behind them.

Slithe shouted directions. "Avoid their bites. Watch for their jumps. Whatever you do, don't get tangled in their threads."

Gruhnt emitted an open-mouthed roar that rumbled the ground. He charged into the mess of jumping spiders. Swinging his iron mace in great swipes and arcs, Gruhnt knocked several of the beasts away from him.

Slithe grinned at an opportunity and rushed toward one of the spiders that landed near him. With a quick, decisive stab, Slithe ran the spider through. He retrieved his weapon and slashed through the spider's hairy body. It squeaked and squealed, spinning its flexing mandibles toward Slithe. He struck at them, squirting blood out onto the road.

Kylani let her arrow fly. It jabbed into a spider's forehead, slowing it to a crawl. Kylani withdrew another arrow from her quiver, loaded it, and shot it into the spider's head beside the first one. It fell limp at the roadside.

A stream of fire gushed past Walter's left side. He bounded out of the way to give Tivara's magic a wide berth. Pleasure and determination arched her thin lips into a smile.

Walter hollered next, a long outpouring of bravery, fear, and action. He darted forward. A jumping spider landed next to the dead one, and Walter swung the hunting knife at its head. The spider chirruped and spread its colorful mandibles as it lurched at Walter.

"You're not feeding on me!" Walter brought the hunting knife's tip down into the spider's head.

Another dispensing of Gruhnt's mace sent two more spiders soaring through the morning light. Tivara blasted one with a fireball, and Slithe chased the other spider with his sword.

Walter kicked his opponent to gain some space between them. He swiped the hunting knife at the spider's front legs, amazed at the efficiency the weapon's enchantment gave him. True to the ability to employ the blade at twice the normal speed, Walter stepped forward and tested it to its limits. He stabbed and slashed, blood spewing in all directions. The jumping spider moved no more, and Walter's chest heaved with every breath.

He looked around. Slithe speared the last of the spiders with his sword and sheathed his weapon. Tivara's flames snuffed out. She lowered one paw and licked the other clean. Kylani removed the unused arrow from her bow and replaced it into her quiver. Gruhnt put away his mace and shield.

Blood stained Slithe's and Walter's leather armor. Crimson droplets dripped from Gruhnt's bronze chest plate.

Walter squeezed his knife handle and sank it into the tin scabbard on his belt. After the whoosh of flames, screeching of wounded enemies, and Kylani's bow twangs, the field had not a single sound left to offer.

Walter wondered at the eight jumping spiders lying dead at his party's feet. "That was awesome! Did you see how amazing we were? How we all had a role to play, and we just nailed it?" Walter punched an excited fist into the air.

Tivara smirked. "Mrow. Look who's in love with combat already? Mmm."

Walter pointed at her. "You liked it, too. I saw you."

Tivara simply purred.

Slithe sauntered over and patted Walter's arm. "Good job, kid. Anyone can sell a sword, but not everyone can handle themselves like you did. I'm serious. You're really one of us today."

Walter plastered a magnificent grin on his face. "Then you're going to congratulate me?"

Suspicion puckered Slithe's reptilian features. "For what? Killing one jumping spider?"

"For leveling. I leveled up." Walter propped his hands on his hips. "You're supposed to congratulate me."

Kylani groaned in disbelief.

Tivara reached her arms up over her head, stretching as high as she could. "There's no harm done in it. You succeeded in your first big battle. Congratulations, Walter." Her tail flicked behind her as she rested her arms at her sides.

Kylani huffed and started up the road past Walter and Tivara. "It was one spider."

Gruhnt approached and shook Walter's hand in his massive green mitts. "I'm proud of you, Walter."

Walter tried to keep both feet on the ground. "Thanks, big guy."

Slithe returned to his post at Gruhnt's side. "Congrats, human."

Walter spoke up, sheepish about the group's reaction. "You know, back home, we just shorten it to *grats.*"

Three moans of agony went up around Walter.

He managed a smile. "Things are back to normal, I guess." He checked the corpse of the spider he'd killed. "Ooh, these give you eyes and legs when you defeat them. Aren't any of you going to loot your kills?"

Slithe tossed a green-scaled hand up. "Help yourself."

Tivara eyed Walter as he ran from corpse to corpse, collecting spider's eyes and juicy legs. "Mrrr. You can only carry so much, Walter. One of these days, you're going to overload yourself."

Walter snatched up the last pairs of eyes and legs. "Yeah, eventually. But that's the beauty of having infinite pocket space. I'm only disadvantaged when I tip my inventory weight to over-encumbered."

Slithe licked the air. "It happens faster than you think."

"I hope so." Walter scrambled onto the road and fell into step next to Tivara. He slipped the final spider eye into his pocket. "That'll mean I've gathered a lot of stuff I can use for crafting and selling."

Kylani drifted to the back of the procession again.

They reached a split in the road, and Walter barely glanced at the place names listed on the signpost. Tivara knew where they were going, and he was sure he'd learn what he needed to know along his journey. He might stick around in the big city for a while or take a roc to some entirely new location. Heck, by the time he strolled back through the archway to Babbling Brook, rumors of his greatness might precede him.

A parade, lots of attention from the local girls, and all the corn on the cob he could devour. Walter rubbed his stomach through his leather cuirass. Yep, life was about to get pretty sweet for this former laughingstock.

Gruhnt put a bounce in his step that alarmed Walter due to the size and weight of the ogre-orc involved. The tank turned to Tivara, his thick fingers wiggling. "We're passing close by Battle Rest."

Walter's stomach twisted into a knot. "What's that? Why don't I like the sound of it?"

Tivara hummed a single low note. "It's Gruhnt's village. His family home is there. It's twenty miles away from their old land, but they've been able to rebuild to a comfortable standard."

Walter braced himself. "Why are you excited about being near it again, Gruhnt?"

The ogre-orc raised and lowered himself on the balls of his feet. "I want to stop by and say hello on the way to Robin's Egg."

Walter searched Gruhnt's and Tivara's faces. "Are you sure that's a good idea, buddy? I mean, considering what happened and everything."

Tivara rumbled to life. "Mrow. It'll be fine. We can fit in a brief visit, Gruhnt. But Kantehar entrusted me with this delivery. I want to conclude it and confirm that with him in good time."

Gruhnt skipped ahead of the group, each push-off of his boots shifting the dirt of the road. "Thank you, Tivara!"

Walter sidled up to the Fee'li mage. "I understand Gruhnt wants to catch up with his family, but what kind of situation are we walking into here? What sort of reception are we going to meet with when we show up with him?"

Slithe issued Walter a sidelong look. "Tell me something, newbie. Is Babbling Brook a curse on your whole town or just a coincidental name?"

Walter inched away from Tivara and resigned himself to keeping a little more quiet. "Coincidence, I guess."

Tivara winked at Walter. "It'll be a good visit. You'll see."

Gruhnt waved his arms through the air as he sailed from one footstep to the next. Walter shook his head. *Poor Gruhnt. He's excited to see his family, and they probably don't want anything to do with him after he burned their old village down. They didn't want him around anymore, and he started adventuring in other parts of Gladfire. He's too kind and polite for his own good. Now we're going to pop up on this village's doorstep, and they're gonna spit in our faces. We'll be lucky if they don't draw swords and maces.*

At the next signpost, Gruhnt led the others off the clear path onto a stretch of barely discernible road. Weeds tangled together at its sides and crisscrossed it in the middle. Walter wanted to search the weeds for any usable alchemy ingredients, but the increase in the number of hills around him set him on edge. He kept his hand on his knife handle instead of rifling through the foliage.

The party followed the path's curves, bypassing a left-hand hill, then two on their right. Walter gulped in his dry throat. He was just about to whisper some more worried questions in Tivara's furry, pointed ear when Gruhnt bellowed into the noontime sunshine. He didn't form words so much as announcements of his presence, somewhere between a trumpet and a kettle drum.

Walter cringed and kept walking.

Dozens of the same sounds echoed back from out of sight. Walter's thumb swirled in circles on top of the knife handle. As his group rounded the next hill, they came to face a fifteen-foot wall. Its tightly woven grass blades showed nothing of what lay beyond it. Torches burned despite the time of day, sending up warped bands of heat and specks of soot.

Wide double doors remained shut in the wall's center. A big, green, round face jutted up over the wall. The ogre scowled, peering down at the arriving party. He wobbled his head from side to side, making his large jowls swing under his small chin. He rose up even higher and beat his fists against his canvas jerkin. The ogre looked down on his side of the wall. "Gruhnt has returned!"

The ogre grabbed the top of the wall and leaned toward Gruhnt with daggers for eyes. "Where've you been?"

Chapter 5

Walter labored to draw his next breath. How many angry, blaming ogres and orcs prepared for battle behind those walls? How many would reach for torches, planning to teach Gruhnt an important and painful lesson in fire safety? How long before the horns of war resounded through these hills and the doors flew open to the most frightening sight Walter had ever seen?

The ogre lookout smacked the butt of his fist on top of the wall. He broke into a welcoming smile. "Blast it, get these doors open! Our hero's come home to us."

Walter held his eyes closed in a long blink. "Hero?"

Gruhnt ducked his chin and dug the toe of his enormous boot into the soil. "I'm only here for lunch. Duty calls me to Robin's Egg."

The ogre at the top of the wall extended his index finger toward Gruhnt. "And somewhere bigger after that, I'll wager."

Gruhnt nodded. "We're off to the Crimson Jewel."

The ogre wiped a tear from under his eye. "I thought so. You make us all proud, Gruhnt. Not many of us have traveled that far."

The double doors sprang wide open. A female ogre jogged out, throwing her arms around Gruhnt. She laughed, her blue eyes sparkling. Cutouts in her oatmeal-colored dress exposed her broad shoulders, and a black cord draped around her thick waist. An eight-foot-tall orc strutted out behind her, offering Gruhnt a firm, hearty handshake.

Walter found his voice first, stammering. "Gruhnt, are these your parents?"

The ogre-orc dried his eyes on the backs of his hands. "Yes, Walter. This is my mother, Urgha, and my father, Tyronus."

Walter stared into their joyous faces. More orcs and ogres poured out of the village doors, giggling and cheering for Gruhnt's return. "I don't understand. I thought, when you told your story about the village fire, that you had a part in causing it."

The orcs and ogres exploded into uproarious guffaws. Only Walter's total confusion kept their enjoyment from squashing his ego.

Urgha laid a hand on her son's arm. "No. The fire was a mistake. Some children were chasing each other, and they knocked one of our torches over. If more of our adults had been there, they might've been able to put it out before it collapsed everything we'd built."

Walter swept his unruly hair back from his forehead. "But Gruhnt told us what happened with so much remorse. Such regret."

Tyronus stood up tall and straight. He clasped his hands in front of him. His voice rumbled deep like a rake dragging through gravel. "Gruhnt cares deeply for every living soul in our community. Almost by himself, he saved every child who otherwise, without his help, would've surrendered to the flames."

Gruhnt tucked his head down and wrapped his big hand around Walter's shoulder. "I almost didn't get to all of them in time, Walter. That's what I was going to say when emotions prevented me from speaking further. The fire trapped several children under a bridge. I had to drench myself in the water just to reach them."

Tyronus regarded his son with pride beaming in his iron-grey eyes. "My son carried all our children to safety. Our village might've burned, but when the rest of us returned home, our entire community awaited us. Out of tragedy, yes, a hero was born."

Urgha let out a pleasant sigh. "And for our meal, a hero's lunch." She pulled on Gruhnt's arm. He bent down on one knee, and Urgha kissed him on the cheek.

Walter sat in the middle of the long table, shaded by an open-sided burlap tent. Tivara rested on his left, and Slithe's muscular form lingered along the right side of Walter's peripheral vision. Kylani remained as motionless as a dead spider at the foot of the table beside Tivara. Seated at the table's head, Gruhnt licked his lips as he considered the bowls and plates of food filling the center of the grey stone surface. His parents occupied the chairs opposite Walter. Urgha, next to her son, scooped large helpings of boiled potatoes and salad greens onto his plate.

Gruhnt grinned without a care in the world. "Thank you, Mother."

Urgha patted his knee. "So, what's this important task that takes Gruhnt all the way to the Crimson Jewel?"

Tivara spread a burlap napkin across her lap. "We're making a delivery for an old friend of mine from when I was studying magic. Gruhnt's already proved a powerful help. Eight jumping spiders ambushed us on the road from Hustle Hub. One swing from Gruhnt's mighty mace sent a handful of them flying."

Tyronus waved toward himself. "Let's see old Blood Fury, shall we, son?"

Gruhnt produced his iron mace and passed it to his father.

Tyronus examined it, rotating the weapon in his hands. "This hefty number's won a fair share of fights. But it wouldn't surprise me if you traded it in for an upgrade sometime this year."

Gruhnt hoisted up his bronze shield. "I already treated myself to this piece of defense when we were in Hustle Hub."

Urgha took the shield and propped it up in her lap, obscuring her from Walter's view. "Very fine craftsmanship, son. You don't buy often, but you buy quality. That's what matters."

Tyronus' eyes met Walter's. "Do you know the orc custom of naming our weapons?"

Walter dotted his napkin to his lips to busy his hands. "No, sir."

Tyronus burst into a full grin. "You have good manners like my son. He gets that from Urgha. From me, he gets the custom of naming his instruments of violence. This one, he calls Blood Fury. Before that, he wielded Blood Feud. And before that, Shining Death."

Urgha set the bronze shield in the grass beside her and leaned it against the table's edge. "Tyronus, you'll scare the human."

Walter hid his trembling hands under the table. "No, I appreciate the lesson, ma'am. Having Gruhnt's battle savvy and strength on the road with us provides a lot of comfort."

Gruhnt's cheeks turned rosy.

Walter picked up his simple, two-tined iron fork. "I do have a question, if you don't mind. If Gruhnt is such a hero and a supporter of your village, why does he go out adventuring?"

Tyronus fell serious and rested his meaty fists on the tabletop. "My son saved dozens of lives when he was merely a teenager himself. As for us adults, we learned our lesson upon our return. We swore never again to endanger our community by spreading our numbers so thin. Exploring, trading, mining, and gathering to the best of our capabilities isn't as important as keeping our families alive. We've kept our promise, and every one of us has encouraged Gruhnt to spread his service to the world. Why hold him hostage here when he can serve the greater good in all of Gladfire?"

Kylani shifted with discomfort in her seat. The rest of the table applauded Gruhnt. He beamed and bowed over the table.

Tyronus reached across the table and covered Tivara's paw with his hand for a moment. "Thank you for befriending Gruhnt and providing him company on the road."

Urgha nodded. "It's made it easier for Gruhnt to leave his family for weeks at a time."

Walter offered a wobbly smile to Tivara. "Yeah, she's good at befriending lonely, away-from-home types."

Tivara licked a lock of Walter's hair. He felt it arcing up at an odd angle off the side of his head. Those seated around the table laughed. Even Kylani, behind knotted arms, managed a sound of amusement.

Hours later, back on the road, Walter walked with a song in his heart and a piping-hot lunch fit to burst out of his stomach. He whistled in idle patches, stopping only to remark, "Your parents are very nice, Gruhnt."

The ogre-orc hummed with appreciation. "Thank you, Walter. The world isn't always friendly to ogres or orcs, but my mother always said that was no reason for us to be impolite."

As the sentiment sank in, Walter nodded. "That makes a lot of sense. I bet if our moms ever met, they'd become the best of friends."

Gruhnt chuckled deep in his chest. "I'd like that."

Walter patted his stomach, which resulted in a warning ache. He winced and took his hand away. "My ma makes this incredible blue-mushroom ravioli. If you're ever near Babbling Brook, you have to stop by and have a plate. It dyes your whole mouth cobalt for the rest of the–"

Walter's jaw dropped almost to the ground.

Nestled in a shallow dip between hills stood a small city. A thick stone wall formed a protective ring around it in a rough oval shape with bump-outs and lookout towers. Someone had painted *Robin's Egg* in clear, blue letters on a huge wooden sign above the open gates.

Walter blew a shrill, impressed whistle.

Slithe chuckled. "Is that what it takes to shut you up, kid?"

Walter marveled at what he saw through the parted gates. Hanging lanterns, bustling crowds, colorful banners. Haggling, threats, and invitations floated on the air. So did the scents of steaming vegetables and brewing potions. Walter's stomach flipped, and he pinched his nose shut.

Gruhnt gave Walter a sympathetic smile. "I overeat every time I'm in Battle Rest, too."

Slithe wrapped his arm around Walter's shoulders. "Come on. We'll hit a few shops, then we'll fly out to the Crimson Jewel. Right?"

Tivara issued a few businesslike nods.

Secured up against Slithe's solid side, Walter strutted into Robin's Egg. Big, bright letters and symbols filled the shop signs. Multiple streets converged into one large intersection, promising more of the same chaos down each of their packed avenues. Few bypassers wore the rough-spun shirts, simple leggings, and muted-hued skirts of the farmlands. A trio of women chittered in cotton dresses dyed rose, periwinkle, and chiffon. Their necklines scooped halfway down their chests, and they compared the wares in their shopping baskets as they swept past Walter. In all the bustle, Walter didn't know where to fix his attention.

Slithe smirked at him. "You're a long way from home, huh, kid?" The Repter withdrew his arm from Walter's shoulders. "See you at the roc point. I've got errands to do."

Slithe slithered off down one road, and Kylani slipped away in another direction.

Gruhnt pointed up at the top of the tallest building reaching up from the city's center. "I'll be waiting for you." He struck off into the thick of the crowd and the marketplace.

Walter scratched his head at Tivara. "I guess that leaves the two of us. I'll just follow you if that's all right."

The mage flipped her hood down and guided Walter down one of the avenues. "Mrow. It's fine."

"Do you know where I can sell some of the ingredients I picked up on the road? I don't think I'm going to cook up spider's legs anytime soon."

"Of course."

Walter glanced around, surprised the rest of their team had disappeared so quickly. "I can't believe every time we're in a town, our party breaks up like this. We seemed so close and cohesive on the journey here."

Tivara paused outside a shop's entrance. "Group members come and go, Walter. That's the way it is."

Something in the middle of Walter's chest ached, and he pondered it. "Maybe. I guess I can't imagine saying goodbye to any of you for good. Kylani, perhaps. Maybe I'll never see Slithe again. But you and Gruhnt... Do you quest regularly? I'd like to work with you some more."

Tivara's lips arced in a patient grimace. "The delivery hasn't even been made yet."

"I know. I mean when this quest is done. Can I travel with you where you're going?"

"We'll see, but there's not much point in it. As I explained to Tyronus at lunch, Gruhnt and I are only making a delivery and reporting back to the mage who trusted it to us. Not every mission is about saving the world."

Walter sighed.

Tivara patted his arm and opened the shop's door. Walter glanced up at the signboard. Unexpectedly, it pictured a drop of blood falling from the tip of a short blade. *The Piercing Lunge* read the thick, scrolling letters beneath it.

Walter followed Tivara inside. "I didn't envision you patronizing this kind of place. Looking for a new backup weapon?"

She purred. "Indeed."

Tivara gravitated toward the counter and the dark-skinned man behind it. Walter occupied himself with the many short-bladed weapons displayed on the walls of the shop. A gold dagger with a mahogany handle made him slack-jawed with its precision and beauty. He reached out to touch the fine tip of a rhodium needle-like stiletto. The sign's image reared like a warning in his head, and Walter reeled his hand back. He had no wish to prick his skin open and bleed on merchandise he couldn't afford.

One of Tivara's wordless sounds trilled behind him. "Ready to go and sell your spider legs?"

Walter cast a longing look over the myriad of short swords and knives resting on wall pegs. "On one condition. You show me what you bought."

Tivara shook her head in wonderment. "Come on."

Walter shadowed her into the street and a few shops down. A sign hung from iron chains in the middle of the front window. *Stuff, Things, and Other Gadgets.* The carving showed a tankard, a bucket, and a small pile of round objects. Walter couldn't tell whether they were marbles, rocks, or eyeballs. In any case, this shop seemed to fit his needs.

The rat-man proprietor stood in the middle of his sales room, hanging pots and pans from hooks around a square stone column. Dark-grey fur covered his portly, short frame. He greeted Walter and

Tivara with fast twitches of his whiskers. "Is that a spider's leg I smell?"

Walter grinned. "I have a few dozen of them I'd like to sell."

The rat-man pushed up his olive shirtsleeves. "Are they fresh?"

Walter dug several of them out of his pocket. "Do they get any fresher than that? We killed the jumping spiders earlier today."

The rat-man's tiny black eyes popped into wide saucers. He scooped up silver coins from a deep pocket in his black leather apron. "I'll take every one you've got."

Walter hoisted the lot of black-and-white striped spider legs from his possession. He traded them for the rat-man's coins and counted the silver with growing excitement. "This is awesome! Thank you so much."

The rat-man eyed his apron pouch full of spider legs. "Thank *you*. Dinner. Tomorrow's lunch, tomorrow's dinner, tomorrow's snack..."

Walter preceded Tivara out of the shop. "Everybody's interested in something different in Gladfire, aren't they?"

Tivara's spacey eyes blinked and returned to their usual observant focus. "Sometimes."

"What's wrong?"

Tivara licked her paw and used it to rub a spot on her forehead. "If case you haven't noticed, I'm a Fee'li. It takes significant willpower not to revert to total cat mentality and plan my own dinner, lunch, and snack when I'm that close to a Rodae. While he was drooling over the spider legs, I was trying not to notice the tenderness of his substantial belly."

Tivara smoothed back her grey-and-black fur. "All right, enough of that. If there's nothing else you need, let's go meet the others."

Walter fell into step with Tivara. "There's nothing left except our bargain, eh? I want to see what you bought at the Piercing Lunge."

Tivara bristled. "Why?"

"So I can live vicariously through you. Let's admit it. The last new weapon I acquired was a hand-me-down, a very generous gift from a shifty but encouraging fighter-thief."

"I appreciate your point." Tivara produced a blade from under her robe. She passed it to Walter and lifted her hood up onto her head.

Walter examined the weapon. Its pale-grey metallic sheen flashed in the sunlight. "Is that real silver?"

Tivara hummed to herself. "Mrrr. Possibly."

Walter laughed. "Did you treat yourself? Did you go all out?"

Tivara shrugged. Her eyes twinkled. "I deserved it, and I had the money."

"Making deliveries really earns you that much coinage?" Walter ran his fingertips along the weapon's red, cherry-wood handle. He returned the item to its owner.

Tivara secured it under her shifting brown robe. "I've performed many services for many creatures. I worked in a hospital for several years before I returned to helping my fellow mages."

Walter dodged a hirsute, hulking man leading a donkey up the street. "I've heard very little about hospitals. We didn't have one in Babbling Brook. Just a few potion brewers and healers we trusted when we got kicked by a goat or took a tumble off the roof."

Tivara took the next left and rubbed her paws together. "You must understand, Walter, that when you seek to compare the schools of magic and rank them, you minimize all of it. Each of them has its place in the world. Each of them perform their good. That's never more evident than in a great battle or healing someone in a hospital."

A shop door flew open on Walter's right, and a gaggle of squabbling children poured out toward the street. He hurried past so they wouldn't crash into him. "Go on."

Tivara took her time to collect her thoughts. "If someone's been burned like the orcs and ogres once were in Gruhnt's home village, they don't need more fire from me. They need ice. If someone has exposure from being out on a mountaintop all night, they need my warmth or perhaps a brief bolt of electricity to jolt them awake. Only nature magic can lift a curse placed by a necromancer. All of it has its place and importance, Walter. You'll never find which one is the most advantageous because that kind doesn't exist."

Walter sank his hands into his pockets and nodded. The road widened into a small, shadowed square. Off to one side, a swirling mass of creatures hunched in front of a burlap bulletin board covered in bounties and notices. "What are they so upset about?"

He walked over and squinted through the throng at a large page tacked over several others. A bold, black headline glared from the top: *Dangerous Necromancer Captured!* Walter leaned in to read more in the paragraph below. *Held as a political prisoner in Lockspire gard, Morattidus faces serious charges of using death magic to threaten and coerce public figures. Investigators have discovered evidence of him employing his magic even against members of his own family. Rest assured, dear citizens, Morattidus is watched closely every second of each day, and he poses no more concern to the good of Gladfire. He awaits his trial and our justice, which are approaching soon.*

Tivara hovered behind Walter's shoulder. "What is it? Mrrm?"

Walter tipped his head toward the announcement. "They're worried about the necromancer, I think."

"Is there one on the loose?"

"He's been caught and taken to some place called Lockspire."

"Slithe might've heard of it."

"You haven't?"

Tivara pursed her lips. "I live on the right side of the law. Those who don't often learn all they can about the prisons that can hold them if they're caught."

"Makes sense." Walter moseyed away from the signboard with Tivara at his side. "So, death magic... what they call necromancy... can you name me one good thing it can do for anyone?"

"In the hospital, it was used to kill pain. It can keep poison from spreading. It can rob a tumor of what gives it nourishment."

Walter clapped. "Tivara, you know the answer to everything."

Tivara's mouth squirmed as she fought a smile. "Almost everything. There are still things I don't know."

Walter swept his hair off his forehead, searching the stone buildings around them. "I don't know where we are or where we're going to meet the others."

Tivara aimed a paw at the sky. "Up, as Gruhnt indicated."

Walter peered up at the eight-story building they headed for. "I've never even seen a roc up close, let alone ridden one. Grandpa would talk about them sometimes, if I mentioned seeing one soaring high above our house."

A small object fluttered over the edge of the building's high roof. At first, Walter wondered if someone had dropped or thrown something. Blood rushed into his muscles in case he needed to dodge it. It twirled down, floating to the left, then easing to the right. As it sank closer to the ground, its magenta color grabbed Walter's curiosity. Its true size also revealed itself, until Walter realized he was watching a two-foot-long feather land on a group of people traipsing through the market. They brushed the feather off onto the street, where Walter ran up to it.

He crouched down and brushed his palm against the feather's blade. Its barbs separated at his touch and met again as his hand moved on. "Is this from the roc?"

Tivara paused her walking. "Yes. It's one of the smaller feathers."

"Smaller?" Walter gripped the feather's white shaft in his hand and tried to tap his thumb against his middle finger. They didn't quite reach.

"Sometimes the roc keepers don't catch the feathers in time and they drift down. Leave it, and someone will retrieve it."

Walter stood up and wiped his hands on his leather cuirass. "Say, how dangerous is roc travel? How many crashes a year? How many casualties? And is it as terrifying as I suspect it is?"

Tivara's paw motioned Walter to keep moving with her up the street. "It's perfectly safe, to answer your questions. Although the height to which rocs climb – and their size and speed – can be off-putting to describe it mildly. Mrow."

The shadow of the roc's building engulfed Walter in its dim coolness. A broad sign above the door captured the outline of a bird in flight, its wings outstretched. A single word beneath it was all the explanation warranted: *Roc.*

The duo entered a plain, rectangular room. A large, hunter-green rug warmed the center of the floor. Half a dozen marble benches supported travelers both bored and chattering. Walter and Tivara climbed flight after flight of flagstone steps, circling the room's four walls that never seemed to stop. Walter glided his hand along the round wooden railing the first few passes. Halfway up, he gripped the railing and released it with sheer trepidation. Sweat pushed out through his forehead, and he sometimes missed at swallowing.

Walter peeked over the railing at the room falling further and further below. His fingers locked around the rail. "Uh, Tivara, I know you'll laugh at this, but the tallest building in Babbling Brook is two and a half stories."

Tivara remained focused on climbing the stairs. "Just keep coming up, Walter. And keep yourself from glancing down."

"I already did. That's my problem."

"Ah, well. Rrrow. What is it that you value most in the world?"

"Adventuring." Walter forced himself up another step to yet another landing. He propped himself up in the corner of the room to catch his breath.

"I believe that means braving heights and taking risks. Wouldn't you agree, hmmr?"

Walter sucked a breath in and let it escape through his mouth. He sized up the steps straight ahead of him. "Adventure, here we come." He fixed his eyes only where they needed to be and set his legs into perpetual motion.

Before Walter knew it, no more stairs lurched into view. Across the landing from him, a ladder rose up through a rectangular hole in the ceiling. By the white wisps streaking through a vastness of blue, Walter surmised they'd reached the roof.

Tivara climbed up, and Walter scrambled up after her. Breezes stirred in his hair that had eluded him on the ground. But it wasn't the wind that arrested his astonishment.

Nestled inside a gigantic nest, the roc radiated color and might. Although its body rested, its goldenrod eyes perceived everything and missed nothing. Its long, gold beak shone in the unadulterated sunlight. Feathers emblazoned its head in the same magenta color as the one that had molted to the street. Behind that block of brightness, other hues cascaded in rings and chevrons over the bird's body. Orange, green, cyan, and scarlet.

At once, the roc shot its wings out to its sides, straight and rigid. A few travelers trekked up the near wing to the bird's back, where a section of sixteen wooden seats had been fastened with thick leather belts. Walter finally took enough of his attention off the roc to find one of its keepers giving it hand signals.

Walter turned and spotted the rest of his traveling party crossing the roof toward him and Tivara. He rubbed the back of his neck. "Until now, Gruhnt was the biggest creature I've seen. Now the roc has so completely blown my mind, I didn't even notice the big guy was already up here."

Gruhnt melted into a kind smile. "No offense taken, Walter."

Tivara gestured to the roc. "We'd better get on. We can talk on the flight."

Another roc keeper approached them, a Cantia man with woolly brown fur. "Pay your fares, please."

Everyone reached into their pockets, but Walter held his hand out to stop them. "How much is it for the five of us?"

"One hundred silver."

Walter rummaged through his pockets for every last coin he carried. He counted them out, finding just enough to cover the cost. Although very little money remained, Walter dropped his earnings into the Cantia's outstretched paws. "Because I can afford it, I'll gladly foot the bill this time. Thanks to Grandpa's sword, Slithe's hunting knife, and one ravenous rat-man."

The Cantia keeper waved the party on. Walter felt a bit strange stepping onto the shifting feathers running down the center of the roc's left wing. It held sturdy even under all their weight, including Gruhnt's.

The seats were arranged in a four-by-four pattern. Kylani lunged for the back row and wedged herself between an existing passenger and the rope strung around the exterior of the platform. Tivara chose the second row, and Gruhnt filed in behind her. Walter followed, and Slithe settled in on his left.

Walter furrowed his brow and tossed a glance back at Kylani. She gazed across the sky away from him, either bored or impatient. "Why does she even bother to travel with us at all?"

Slithe made a slurping sound. "Want of money makes creatures do strange things."

The roc keepers ushered several more travelers up the roc's wing to the seating platform. They filled in the empty chairs in the front row and a few behind Walter. With all the seats taken, the keeper closest to the roc threw his hand up. The roc tucked its wings in and stood up. The platform remained steadier than Walter anticipated, but its swaying still shot panic through his stomach.

Walter managed a pathetic grin. "Gosh, with all this open sky up here, you'd think there'd be more air to breathe."

Slithe had no problem baring his teeth in a wide, entertained smile. "It's quite the opposite, actually, especially for your first roc flight."

The huge bird extended its wings and flapped them hard. The platform rose, jostling Walter back against the support of his chair. His inner organs sloshed and traded places. The bird gained altitude, and Walter thought he was about to lose his lunch.

He groaned and scrunched his eyes shut. *Don't think about food. I must be turning green.*

He gulped. *I must be immeasurably, inexplicably stupid to let them talk me into this. I mean, I hardly know them. They're basically four strangers I met yesterday.* Late *yesterday, at that.*

Walter squeezed his thighs, his fingernails digging through his leggings into his skin. *I'm the worst kind of gullible. All Tivara had to do was mention adventuring, and I rashly followed her all the way up here. Now I'm riding on a bird the size of my family home!*

He pushed air in and out of his mouth. Or was it pulling itself in and out? *Tivara tricked me into this! A cat-woman who less than half an hour ago had to restrain herself from eating the rat-man I sold my spider legs to!*

Walter's throat sealed up, and fear of suffocation prompted him to take one big gasp for breath. His eyes opened, round with panic. And what he saw was the opposite of his internal nightmare.

Slithe relaxed next to him with zero protection between himself and falling to his death. In fact, in the event of any trouble, Slithe would possibly save Walter's very life by tumbling off the platform first. Walter wouldn't have sold his grandfather's sword and been able to treat his party to this ride if Slithe weren't so hospitable with the enchanted knife.

On Walter's other side, Gruhnt's muscular frame extended beyond the confines of his chair. Gruhnt had been nothing but gracious and giving since Walter met him in Wanderer's Respite.

At the end of the row sat Tivara, obscured completely by Gruhnt's massive form. Walter's head drooped. He ought to be ashamed of himself for blaming anything but good fortune on the mage. She'd agreed to let him partner up with them despite his minimal skills, and she'd travailed to educate him on nearly every subject he'd raised to her.

Even Kylani riding in the back apart from them. She'd gifted Walter with an enchanted ring when she didn't have to.

These weren't strangers. These were his friends, and he'd meant what he'd said to Tivara in the marketplace. He didn't expect to stay in contact with all of them forever, but he couldn't fathom walking away from his party without a second thought.

And beyond them, past the other travelers, and above Walter's head, stretched the eternal Gladfire sky. Deep and peaceful and blue.

Walter stared into it. "Wow."

Slithe looked up as well. "I once bought a piece of topaz this same color."

Walter struggled to enunciate in his dream-like state. "Did you?"

"No. I stole it."

"I guess I shouldn't be shocked." Walter observed the unhurried wafting of the clouds. "Speaking of thieving, I have a question about Lockspire gard."

Slithe jerked. "What? Why?"

"There's a prisoner who's been jailed there. Tivara and I read about it in the marketplace."

"What about it?" Heavy waves of tension rippled off Slithe.

Walter studied him, stumped. "I don't know. Is it secure? Is it good at doing what it's supposed to do?"

"Keep creatures locked up? Yeah. It's got some of the tightest security measures in this part of Gladfire."

"Tivara told me you might know something about that place."

"Yeah, I keep it as a reminder." Slithe held up three scaly fingers. "Don't get captured. Those are the words I live by. You end up in Lockspire, you're not seeing the sun again until the duke says you can."

"So we're probably safe from the necromancer the guards rounded up?"

"If he's in Lockspire, he's in a worse predicament than we are, kid."

"Is it worse than free-falling onto the iron part of a bridge?"

Slithe stroked his beard of pointy scales. "According to what I've heard, it's a lot like that. Every single day."

The roc and the platform dipped. Walter's stomach lifted, but he clung to his newfound trust of the roc's ability. The bird glided down in a smooth arc and perched on top of a building where Walter could still only see the infinite sky. The roc stepped forward into the provided nest and settled in. It propped its wings out, and the first row of passengers filed off the platform.

Tivara leaned past Gruhnt to look at Walter. "How are you holding up?"

Walter popped his thumb up out of his fist. "My lunch is right where I put it in Battle Rest."

"Good boy."

Slithe got up, and Walter followed suit. The party rematerialized around Walter, and they moved for the open hatch in the red terracotta roof leading into the building they stood on.

Walter took one last gander from this height, no other buildings rivaling this one. "Hey, Tivara. Do you know how many stories tall this roc nest is?"

"Twenty."

Walter pitched forward as if a rug had been yanked from beneath his boots. "Thanks for telling me."

Slithe aimed a flat hand at the hatch's opening, and Walter scampered down the ladder ahead of the others. They made their way down all the stairs to the lobby and emerged into a cacophony of packed action.

A human woman leaned against the opposite building. She bent her knee and propped her boot sole against its bricks. Her straw-blonde hair hung in greasy curls around her painted face. Her cackling laugh percussed along the paved street, showing the gaps in her crooked teeth. The short sleeves of her mustard dress draped from her thin shoulders, and the hem of its skirt only covered the top halves of her thighs.

She set a fingertip into her chin dimple as she regarded the newly arrived party. "Here are some lonely lads, surely? Thirty silver a go. And I'll do certain things those snobbish women won't."

Walter hung back, glued to the doorframe. His companions remained around him.

A Cantia guard in a crimson uniform rounded the corner. He brushed the woman away. "Move on. Go back to your own neighborhood. These fine folk don't want anything you've got."

The woman pointed. "You don't know that! And it's a mixed neighborhood here anyway on account of the roc's nest. You don't know what kind of creatures are gonna step off that platform."

The guard drew a black-wood club. "It's your last warning. Go home."

The woman sneered and pushed off from the wall. "I'll go, but he don't know what you came hungry for, does he, fellas?" She wobbled on her feet but limped away out of sight. "Those who seek me out always find me."

The Cantia guard harrumphed and strung his club off his belt. He spread his arms open to Walter and his friends. "Travelers, welcome to the greatest city in all of Gladfire. The Crimson Jewel!"

Chapter 6

Another hulking, solidly built shoulder slammed into Walter's. He resigned himself to it and rubbed the potential bruise with his hand. A wooden shop door swung open and cracked against the wall of its building. A Repter man flew out of the entrance, landing in a sprawl on the front walk.

The orc proprietor loomed in the doorway, wiping his hands against each other in intimidating slices "Don't try to haggle me that low again. You won't get off so easy."

Walter grimaced.

Whoops and coos lured Walter's glance to the other side of the street. Three young women, two humans and a Fee'li, fanned their rosy faces.

The tall one in the middle shook her head of curly ginger hair. "Ooh, they must be new. I'd remember if I'd seen them before." She nibbled her fingernail.

The petite blonde beside her tugged on the long braids snaking down to her waist. "Are you sticking around long, fellas? My friend here is single. In need of a husband." She pointed to the redhead.

Walter gave the trio his full attention. "We won't be here..."

The two human women's blouses sagged off their shoulders, the blonde's tanned bronze and the redhead's milky pale. Straps from their skirt waistbands held the brown fabric's fullness a few inches above their knees. The blonde's red wool stockings and her friend's green tights drew Walter's eyes. Their Fee'li companion snickered beside them in a purple tank top and short khaki-green shorts showing off grey-fur-covered legs.

Walter shielded his vision from the strangers and blushed hot. He picked up his pace. "We're not staying. Gosh. My mum would not approve of me seeing so much of a woman before I'm married."

Slithe slung his arm around Walter's shoulders. "Then you're in luck. That's what she's looking for." Slithe descended into guffaws.

Walter sprang a wary eye on Tivara, desperate for sympathy. "Is this really the best city in the world?"

Tivara considered their surroundings. The buildings held more architectural styles than Walter had ever seen in one place. A bigger variety of materials constructed them than he'd known existed. Every roof was made of curved, red terracotta tiles or gleamed with copper's red-gold sheen. "It's a good city but complicated. Calling it the greatest is certainly an opinion, not a polled consensus."

Walter turned back to Slithe, who had finally sobered. "What do you see here?"

Slithe licked at the air with his forked tongue. "Opportunity." He let Walter go.

Walter tugged at his shirt collar, finding it hot and uncomfortable. "How long are we staying in the Crimson Jewel?"

Tivara strolled the crowded street with purpose. "That's up to you, young Walter. Once our delivery is executed, I'll pay all of you for your participation, and you're free to go your own way."

Walter nibbled the inside of his lip.

Tivara sighed. "Or accompany Gruhnt and me back to the mage school."

Walter blew out a breath of relief. "Thanks, Tivara."

Gruhnt patted him on the back. "We're glad to have you along, Walter."

Tivara scoured the area around them. "We're looking for a garden. That's where our contact is supposed to meet us. It has two tall statues in it of the city's founder and its master builder."

Gruhnt lifted a flat hand above his eyes to shade them. "I don't see it on this street."

Tivara's paw patted a quick rhythm on the side of her leg. "Perhaps we're close." She took a left, and the others followed her.

Gruhnt pointed ahead and to the right. "We're almost there."

The group pushed its way through the fracas of travelers and locals. They stepped into the garden, overflowing with verdant plants and bright flowers. Its dozen trees ranged from saplings to thirty feet tall. The wood-and-iron benches held very few creatures.

A Fee'li woman with orange fur watched two cat-children batting at a fountain's waterfalls. A young moss elf picked a spray of small, vermillion cardinal flowers, a few shades lighter than his garnet eyes. He offered the blooms to the elven lady beside him, and she hugged them up against her chest.

Walter noted a swell of cardinal flowers to his left, growing in an urn-shaped terracotta planter. He danced his fingers down their stems to pick them.

Tivara's paw batted him away. "We're not here to harvest their garden. We're just looking for our contact."

Walter left the cardinal flowers alone and resolved to pick twice as many on the road. "Do we have a name or description?"

"Rrrrm, yes. Noraddian. He's short and well-dressed."

"You don't know what race he is?"

The rest of the party fixed sharp glares on Walter.

He held his palms up to steady his group mates. "I didn't mean anything by it. I was just asking so I'd know who to look for."

Slithe emitted a long, quiet hiss. "Trying to separate the fur from the scales, as it were?"

Walter squeaked. "Yes."

Tivara exhaled. "I don't know. I didn't ask. Kantehar didn't divulge that information."

Walter moved to put a little extra distance between Slithe and himself. His fingers plucked at one of the cardinal flower leaves. "Do we know his eye color or anything like that? Some sort of passcode?"

"No. I told Kantehar I'd bring the delivery into the city today." Tivara sat down on a nearby bench. "He assured me he'd send word for Noraddian to meet us here. We might as well make ourselves comfortable and wait."

Kylani rested her back against a sturdy tree trunk. Gruhnt settled into a patch of grass and folded his long legs. Slithe eased himself onto a bench neighboring Tivara's, and Walter remained by the vase of cardinal flowers. He didn't roam this far from home to sit around, after all.

The two moss elves wandered off, hand in hand. As the sun slipped behind the city's tallest roofs, the mother Fee'li called to her children. She led them off, grabbing hold of their paws with hers.

A short, stocky figure whisked into the garden. Walter bolted upright, his heart fluttering with hope. The dwarf sported a greying brown beard that tapered to his ankles. Instead of fancy clothes, he wore a dirty, coal-stained apron. Beneath it, he layered a rough-spun collared shirt and thick burlap pants. A hole the size of a silver coin was half worn through one boot above the toes. Walter deflated, and the dwarf hurried on his way across the garden.

Walter gestured after him. "I thought he was our guy."

Tivara stretched her legs out and let her feet drop to the ground again. "Keep looking."

Slithe rolled his head on his neck. "How long do we wait?"

"I'm not sure. Noraddian was supposedly eager for this delivery. Kantehar told me he'd sit in the garden all day if he had to so he wouldn't miss us."

"May I inquire the nature of this mysterious delivery?"

"You may ask, but I will not answer. That detail is shared only amongst the few of us involved in its direct handling."

Slithe bowed his head in respect.

Walter surveyed the garden and the streets visible around it. A crew of towering orcs shouldered a foot-wide wooden column through the crowd. Average-height humans, Fee'li, and Cantia passed by in their activities.

Kylani scoffed and peeled away from the tree trunk. "What's plan B? He's not showing up."

Slithe nodded. "I agree. Do you know anything else about this chap?"

Tivara stood up and arced her belly forward to loosen her back. "Not really. But if he's well-dressed, he's wealthy. We'll find that part of the city and locate him."

Walter and the others followed Tivara out of the garden.

She stopped the first creature she spotted with a gold necklace adorning a silk outfit. "Mrow, excuse me. I have an appointment in the shinier part of the city."

The grey-headed Fee'li man rested a paw over his chest, toying with his pendant. His pearlescent blue eyes looked Tivara over. "A fine cat such as yourself surely does."

"Do you know where I might find it? Can you point the way?"

The Fee'li indicated the opposite direction with the tip of his striped tail.

"Thank you." Tivara turned, the rest of the group moving with her.

The Fee'li stranger purred. "I hope I'll see you there."

Tivara scowled and rolled her eyes. "That's all I need," she murmured.

Walter kept pace at her side. "You're not looking for a partner in life?"

"Looking for trouble, you mean. I certainly am not."

The group walked until the stone and maple houses turned to granite and sandstone. Every creature on this new street floated in silk, velvet, and tweed. Gold and silver encircled their necks. Garnets, sapphires, and diamonds glittered from their rings.

Tivara waylaid a Cantia woman with short, dark fur. "Mrrr, begging your pardon. Do you know Noraddian?"

The Cantia woman growled, exposing sharp white teeth. "I never heard of him. Mind where you're going, pussycat." She strode past Tivara, bumping shoulders with her.

Tivara blinked, and her jaw tensed. "What lovely jewels. Too bad they clash with your ugly manners."

Walter pushed his shirt cuffs up. He wanted to run after the Cantia woman and give her a loud talking-to. That would probably end with interference from a guard or one of his travel mates. He redirected his attention to the next creature strolling towards him.

The fox-man's short stature made Walter's heart leap. "Excuse me, sir. Are you, by any chance, Noraddian?"

The Vulyon shook his head. "I've heard the name, though. He's lived in the city a couple of years now."

Walter licked his lips. "Do you know where we might find him? Does he have a house or a shop nearby?"

The Vulyon shifted his whiskers from side to side. He turned away and waved to the other creatures in the street. "Are any of you acquainted with a Mr. Noraddian?"

A female moss elf with eyes like rubies raised her ochre-colored hand. Her other hand held a black fur wrap around her body. "He's a neighbor of mine."

Tivara took a quick step forward. "I have an urgent delivery for him. He's expecting it."

The moss elf tilted her index finger to point loosely behind her. "You can find him at the Golden Silks apartments."

"Thank you."

Tivara darted off, and Walter jogged after her. The others trailed close behind them.

Amidst the two- and three-story houses, a larger building rose ten windows high. Gold flecks sparkled from its smooth sandstone blocks. Balconies sprouted from it, ringed with scrolling silver railings. The group hurried inside. A cranberry-red carpet covered the lobby's floor.

Tivara approached the human man behind the ornate wooden counter.

His mahogany eyes simmered, and the gold ring hanging from his aquiline nose glimmered. He wore no shirt under his red satin vest, displaying muscular arms with a gold band circling each bicep. He offered a sly grin. "Welcome to Golden Silks. How may I be of service to you?"

Tivara swiped her robe's hood down from her head. "I have a special delivery I'm being paid to hand over personally to Noraddian. Can you tell me which apartment is his?"

The raven-haired deskman maintained his coy detachment, passing his eyes over each member of the party. "You'll forgive me if I protect the privacy of our guests."

Walter ambled up to the counter. He flapped his hand dismissively at his friends. "I'm sorry. I'm not with them. I'm a guest of a certain moss elf I think you might be familiar with." Walter wagged his eyebrows up and down. He leaned his forearms on the counter. "Her wealth is only exceeded by her beauty, if you know what I mean."

The deskman bowed at the waist. "I do, sir."

Walter spied a thick leather book on the lower surface of the counter within the deskman's reach. "Unlike these... peasants... who'd have to thumb through your records to find who they're supposedly searching for, I'm quite expected."

The deskman raised an eyebrow at the blood and soil caked onto Walter's shirt.

"I just returned to the city. Milady passed me in the street in her finest fur, and I aim to set the mood for her before she comes home."

"Excellent, sir."

"If you'll just let me in – it'll only take a moment of your time – I'll see there's a healthy tip in it for you. Then you can continue speaking sense into these... rabble rousers."

The deskman produced a gold key from his vest pocket. "This way, sir."

Walter trailed the man to the ebony staircase. Walter spun around long enough to flash a thumbs-up and point in hasty motions to the leather-bound book. He regained his composure in an instant and shadowed the deskman up to the third floor.

The deskman unlocked the third door on the right and winked. "Best of fortune to you."

"Thank you." Walter paused. What if his compatriots needed more time? He hadn't found any opportunity to discuss a full plan with them. What if his half-cooked idea left him trapped in this strange elf woman's apartment and his friends still didn't meet up with Noraddian?

The deskman slapped the key against his palm several times. "Is there anything else, sir?"

"Do you know where she keeps her best wine cups? Every time I've been here, I haven't paid attention to where she gets them."

The deskman's full lips twisted up into an impish curve. "You might check the kitchen cabinets."

A thin line of fire hugged the wall behind the deskman. Walter stared at it, perplexed. It curled and separated into letters. *Coming up.*

Walter closed his eyes and shook his head. He flung his arm out toward the depths of the apartment. "You're the help here. Help me."

The deskman cocked his head at an unappreciative but respectful angle. "As you command."

He entered the apartment, and the fire letters dissipated into faint black smoke. The deskman headed for the far right-hand area of the living space. Rich, dark wood cabinets lined the kitchen.

Walter closed the door. "And music. We have a little game going where she wants me to guess her favorite kind of music. Do you happen to know how I might win?"

"No, I don't know all the personal details of Miss Faunafloria." The deskman peeked inside each cabinet in turn.

Walter heard footsteps passing by in the corridor. He rotated in a frantic circle, scouring the living area for any musical instruments. Not even a music box decorated any of the tables or shelves.

The deskman perked his head up, his eyes preoccupied.

Walter stomped on the floor and kept stamping until his shins hurt. He set his hands on his hips. "You should really hire someone to keep the bugs out of here."

"I'll keep that suggestion in mind." The deskman carried a pair of delicate wineglasses to the dining table. Pearls and emeralds sparkled from below the rim. "Are these what you wished for, sir?"

Walter huffed out a long breath. "Yes, those will have to do."

"Do you want me to seek out something with which to play music?"

"Uh…" Walter opened the hall door. He let his voice echo through the corridor and up the stairwell. "I don't know if I'll need your assistance anymore or not. I didn't even get your name in case I need to call for you."

The deskman meandered toward Walter. "Silus, sir."

"Very good."

A small ball of flames sank into Walter's view at the end of the hallway. It morphed into an upward-pointing arrow.

Walter gave Silus a bright smile. "I think we're all set, then. Thank you very much."

Silus stepped into the hall.

Walter passed him a few silver coins. "I know milady thanks you, too."

"You're too kind."

Silus slipped away and descended the stairs. Walter sank to his haunches and bit into his fist. He screamed inside his head. *Who am I?*

He breathed himself back into normalcy and got up off the rug. He tucked the two wineglasses into a random cabinet and scurried out of the moss elf's apartment.

Walter tiptoed as fast as he could along the corridor and up the stairs. When he didn't see anyone for several floors, his shoulders drooped. Had his friends left already? Had Noraddian invited them in already? Or had they shut themselves into one of these apartments, and Walter would have to guess which one they hid in?

At the eighth floor, a Cantia couple emerging from their apartment startled Walter. They sniffed the air with small, black noses.

Walter clasped his hands together. "Good evening. I'm a guest of Miss Faunafloria. I'm going up to borrow some wine from you-know-who."

The Cantia woman tugged her cashmere shawl tighter around her slender shoulders. "She always did prefer the commoners. When you have money to throw around, I suppose."

The couple started down the steps, and Walter doubled his pace in ascending them.

On the topmost landing, he noticed one of the doors ajar at the end of the hall. "Thank goodness." Walter speed-walked to it and slid inside the apartment. Cherry wood seemed to make up everything from the furniture and the floors to the countless bookshelves and kitchen cabinets. Walter closed the door with hardly a click. "Noraddian? Tivara?"

Slithe crept out of a shadow in the corner, seizing Walter's heart in a fright. The Repter held up a lockpick. "We made ourselves at home."

"I see. There's no one here?"

Tivara ambled in from another room. She set her satchel on a round, wooden table. "No one who legally belongs here."

Slithe tucked his lockpick away and sent a light punch to Walter's arm. "Smooth lying, kid. You did us all proud."

Gruhnt gazed down at Walter with sad, longing eyes.

Walter spread his hands apart. "I didn't want to, Gruhnt. Honest. It was the only inspiration I got to sneak us past Silus at the desk."

Slithe exhaled a light breath. "You even scored his name. Good job."

"I've learned a lot of things in the last five minutes."

Kylani traipsed in from another doorway. "I thought you were small-town."

"I am." Walter rifled his fingers through his hair. "There was this old, wrinkled guy in Babbling Brook. Farmer Porter. He didn't have much strength left in his thin, saggy arms, but he knew if he swung a good-sized stick, he could put you in a land of hurt."

Kylani lingered at the edge of the main room. "He swung at you?"

"Oh, yeah. Once. He'd take a shot at anybody he caught climbing over his fence without permission."

Slithe spoke up. "Sweet corn?"

Walter patted his stomach. "Berries. Every kind that grows in the Song Lands, he cultivated on his property. And the only thing

Farmer Porter was better at than growing fruit was picking a walloping stick."

Walter formed his thumbs and middle fingers into a complete circle. "It had to be this big around. He'd grab it in both hands and whirl it at you."

Slithe folded his arms. "Slightly entertaining. What's your point?"

"Downstairs, when I realized my best move was to pretend I belonged in this neighborhood at all, I pictured Farmer Porter's hefty stick. I imagined what it would be like to have that jammed up my bumside and be so stodgy, it hurts "

Slithe let his laughter rip. He clapped Walter on the shoulder. "Sometimes, you still surprise me, kid. I'm glad you came along."

Tivara met Walter with a calm, level gaze. "It doesn't solve our problem of making the delivery, I'm afraid."

Slithe laid his hand on the table. "Leave the item here. This Noraddian character will discover it when he gets home."

Tivara's tail twitched behind her. "Kantehar was clear. I'm to pass it straight to Noraddian."

"It's that critical, yet you still can't tell us what it is?"

"I'm sorry. Some of us hold our integrity intact, thief."

Walter wandered away from the discussion, drawn to the bookshelves. He tilted his head sideways to read the words on the leather spines. *History of Gladfire*. *Treaties of the World's Races*. *Anatomy of Fee'li: Humorous Essays and Collected Facts*.

Walter faded and wobbled. These fun and exciting titles almost put him to sleep.

Slithe hardened his voice. "What do you propose we do? This job doesn't pay that well. The longer we wait, the less we're truly being compensated."

Walter blinked hard to wake himself up and tried the lower shelf of volumes. *Gathered Maps of the Song Lands*. *Charts and Courses through the Lovely Leaves and the Mossy Fold*. One tome bore stick-like hand lettering. *Records and Receipts*.

Behind Walter, Tivara hissed. "Don't threaten me, lizard. You have the choice to leave at any time. What you seem to lack, however, is patience."

Walter snatched the record book off its shelf. "Hey, you two. I might've found something."

The book slipped out of Walter's fingers and thumped on the floor. Its pages jumped open, shooting scraps of paper all over the navy rug. Walter froze while the smallest, lightest pages flitted at his feet.

Kylani slapped a hand over her eyes.

Slithe seethed with annoyance, and Tivara's face fell.

Walter dove to his knees. "I'm sorry. I'll fix this."

Gruhnt knelt at Walter's side. "I'll help you, Walter."

Slithe growled and turned his back on them. "What were you thinking? You still have a long way to go before you can undergo this kind of mission on your own."

"Qu-qu-qu-quest," Walter reminded him. He scooped a collection of papers into his hand. "I thought if Noraddian had stored any recent receipts or plans in this book, we might be able to track where he is."

"Damn." Slithe sank into a chocolate-leather armchair. "That's smarter than I assumed."

Gruhnt laid a pile of receipts and notes on the open book pages. "Do you want me to read them with you, Walter?"

Walter peered in wonder and perplexity at the receipt on top of the mound. Confusion clouded his brain so much, he almost couldn't form it into words. He picked up the hand-written page. "Since when is corundum as expensive as rhodium?"

Slithe scoffed and threw his hands up.

Tivara tapped her paw pads on the table. "It's not, Walter. Rrrow. I explained the metal ranking system to you in Hustle Hub."

Walter got to his feet and showed the page to Tivara. "Then either I'm an idiot, Noraddian's an idiot, or there's something really fishy going on here."

Slithe and Kylani puffed out aggravated air in unison. "The first one."

The sky elf glowered at the Repter and turned her face away.

Slithe moved toward the receipt with the ghost of a smirk on his lips. "What's it say, exactly?"

Gruhnt looked up with curious eyes.

Walter drew his fingertip under the handwritten lines as he read them. "Sold: twenty-five corundum bars. Cost: twenty-five rhodium bars."

Slithe ran his palm over the prickly scales on top of his head. "The kid's right, mage. There's some dirty business going on."

Walter let Tivara take the receipt from him. "Is there any chance Noraddian doesn't understand metal prices anymore than I did? Maybe he got swindled."

Slithe glanced around at the cherry-wood furnishings and gold lamps. "I've known some creatures who got rich despite being simpletons, but you don't live this high on the hog without enough brain cells to rub together. Perhaps it's Noraddian who's playing a rigged game."

Tivara held up the receipt. "How? Mrow? When the evidence suggests otherwise."

Slithe examined the page. "We don't know what it suggests, sweet lady."

Walter laid a hand on Gruhnt's armored shoulder. "Would you mind looking through the other receipts, big fella? Maybe we can find something else Noraddian bought or sold in the last few days."

Gruhnt nodded and sifted one by one through the papers on top of the open book.

Slithe whopped his knuckle against the receipt in question. "Do you have any reason to suspect Noraddian might be in trouble or causing problems for other creatures?"

Tivara folded her arms over her brown robe. "No. All I have are the instructions I was given for the delivery."

Walter squinted at the myriad of book titles remaining on the shelves. *Creatures of the White Bog. The Heights of Gladfire's Mountains. Fee'li, Cantia, and Other Humanoids.*

Slithe leaned toward Tivara, his height and form greater than hers. "For the last time, I'll ask you. What's your delivery for Noraddian?"

Tivara peered like a cold statue into Slithe's eyes, almost straight through him. "Not. Your. Business. Rrrow."

Walter ran his tongue over his dry lips and searched another shelf of tomes. *The Wealthy's Guide to Home Ordering. The Crimson Jewel's Best Inns and Apartments. Magic à la Carte: Supplementing Your Skills with Spellwork.*

Slithe pounded a fist on the table. "You don't think it's my business now that I'm wasting my time looking for someone who's not here?"

Walter slipped the last book down into his hands. "Hey. I might've found something. It's an instruction manual for strengthening your fighting and trickery skills with specific magic choices."

Slithe laid the puzzling receipt on the table and pinned it down with his index finger. "I don't mess around when it comes to magic. You might understand it, Tivara, but I don't. A lockpick and a blade. That's what I understand."

Tivara lowered her gaze to the ogre-orc still seated on the rug. "Have you found anything, Gruhnt?"

He shook his head.

Tivara leveled her gaze with Slithe's again. "You may stay to help, or you may leave. Those are your options as they have been since you offered your assistance to our group yesterday."

Kylani bit her fingernails.

Slithe advanced an inch toward the mage. "I won't abandon a job I haven't finished, and I won't be paid for a job I didn't do."

Walter flapped the magic book open. "Um, hey, you two. Let's not squabble, eh?" He perused the table of contents and flipped at random into the bulk of pages.

Slithe pointed at Tivara. "Maybe you're being set up, and now we are, too. There is no Noraddian."

Walter held up a finger. "The moss elf in the street knew him."

Slithe retreated to the armchair and sank into it. "He could be dead for all we know. I should go question Silus downstairs and find out what he's hiding."

Tivara bristled. "Interrogate, you mean. Intimidate. I won't allow it on a mission I'm heading up."

Walter jerked a thumb at the bookshelves. "I'm sure if you check out the guide to the city's apartment buildings, it'll tell you the deskman's privacy policy."

Slithe slid down against the armchair's seat. "No, thank you."

Tivara swung desperate eyes on Walter. "Anything in that book?"

Walter shrugged. "I don't know what I'm looking for. I'm not very familiar with spells. Without any other clues, we have no inkling what Noraddian was doing with this information. He could be interested in basic shields or terrible curses."

"It was worth a look."

Walter returned the manual to its shelf beside a small, dark-wood carving of a ball in a decorative stand.

Tivara balked at Slithe. "You won't even get up and help us?"

Slithe hissed. "Maybe I'm waiting until Gruhnt discovers something we can actually follow up on."

"Right now, Walter's done more good than you have in getting to the bottom of what we came here for."

Walter thought he saw something on top of the bookshelf, the pink-and-black marble corner of an object.

Slithe's exhale roared. "Kylani's done less than the rest of us. If you have a problem with the efficacy of this group, address it with her first."

Walter lifted a foot and tested the lowest shelf's sturdiness. It wobbled, but it remained in place.

Tivara growled. "I have no issues with Kylani. Her archery skill aided us during the jumping-spider attack–"

Slithe cut her off. "As did my sword and leadership."

Walter set his foot on the shelf and prepared himself to make a measured jump.

Tivara's voice hardened and grew louder. "–and I must add, Kylani hasn't repeatedly intruded into my private affairs to ask what I've made clear I will not divulge."

Walter leapt up for the mysterious item. His fingers closed around one boxy edge of it as the shelf gave way underfoot. He yelped. His free hand grasped the nearest hold he could find, the statuette shaped like a garden ball on a pedestal.

No! Why didn't I grab the bookshelf itself?

The statuette gave way, and Walter collapsed in a heap into Gruhnt's discarded pile of inspected receipts. The impact loosened Walter's grip on the item collected from the top of the bookshelf, and it clattered away. Walter's lower back ached, and he slowly pushed himself up.

Slithe clapped his hands in a halting rhythm. "Well done, chap. Two disasters in ten minutes."

Walter picked up what he'd dropped, which turned out to be a hefty marble picture frame. He scanned the rug. "Where's the statue?"

He raised his eyes to the bookshelf.

The statuette sat at a sharp angle on the shelf where it had been when Walter reached for it. Beside the bookcase, a section of the wall whooshed open, sliding behind the wall that remained in place. Beyond the new doorway, papers and books filled a large table. Ornate wooden chairs stood around it, upholstered in green velvet.

Walter laughed. "Two disasters or two accidental discoveries?"

Tivara sniffed the air. "I don't smell any creatures hiding in there."

Walter walked into the hidden room. His comrades' clothes and armor shifted as they followed him in with curiosity and caution.

Walter approached the table. "Quest."

Tivara cocked an eyebrow.

"You said *mission* again." Walter set the picture frame down on the table's bare corner. "Who wants to bet what we're looking for is here?"

Five different hands – tanned, fuzzy paws, green, scaled, and white-grey – picked up pieces from the assembled pile.

Tivara hummed deep in her throat. "It's the same kind of notice you and I saw near the marketplace, Walter. About the necromancer Morattidus being taken prisoner in Lockspire."

Kylani showed her page to the rest of the group with a solemn set to her mouth. "There's another flyer about Morattidus, dated six months earlier. When giant wild cats swarmed on his village, they killed his wife."

Tivara took Kylani's flyer and swallowed with a gulp. "This isn't just about Morattidus. It mentions Noraddian."

Walter shook as he lifted the picture frame beside the flyer. The three rat-people captured in the frame's small painting looked identical to the trio of Rodae printed on the flyer. "Not only did we just find out what race Noraddian is, we've found evidence connecting him straight to the most dangerous creature we know of."

Chapter 7

Tivara left her two pages on the large table and walked out of the secret room.

Slithe shot a hand out at her. "We prove your delivery taker is up to no good, and that's your reaction? To save yourself and run away?"

Tivara ambled back in, carrying her satchel. "It's time now I tell you all what I was intended to bring to Noraddian."

She situated her satchel on the table's edge and lifted out a blue velvet bag. She unfastened its drawstring and produced two translucent glass bottles. They flared wide at the bottom and narrowed evenly to coin-sized openings at the top.

Walter peered through one bottle's clear walls at Kylani. "They're empty?"

Slithe tapped a pointed claw on the bottle's shimmering cap. "Potions of invisibility, boy. With the seals still intact."

Walter faced Tivara. "You knew this whole time what was in this bag?"

The Fee'li mage nodded. "Indeed. Kantehar was up-front and honest with me."

Slithe exploded. "About invisibility potions?"

Walter waved his hand for Slithe to calm down. "Tivara, what *legal* reasons could Noraddian have for wanting this type of potion?"

Tivara blew out a fluid breath. "He could want them in combat. He could want them for listening in on a conversation when he had reason to believe he himself were being plotted against."

Slithe jabbed a finger at the portrait in Walter's hand. "There's nothing legal going on here. We've just drawn a straight line between our delivery taker and a jailed necromancer."

Walter rushed into the other room and toted the inexplicable receipt into the hidden room. "Tivara, before you launch into another round of argument with Slithe, it's about time we got back around to the corundum conundrum."

Four pairs of eyes stared deadpan at Walter. Their owners said, "The what?"

Walter grinned and shook the receipt out. "It's about corundum, and it's a bit of a conundrum. What would you call it?"

Slithe sneered at him. "Almost time to go home."

Gruhnt selected a page from the table's maelstrom. He cleared his throat in smooth exhales. "Dear brother-in-law. If Orantia's death had made them listen – actually change their rotted minds – I would've left her buried. My widowing would've led to something good. But with twelve of us lying dead and bleeding in the streets, the duke wouldn't send us the guards to fend off more attacks. If he would've heeded our pleas the first dozen times, none of those Rodae would've perished. I would have my wife, and you would have your beloved sister."

The ogre-orc laid the letter on the table. "It's not signed."

Tivara passed her papers to Walter and accepted the framed picture into her paws. The two rat-men flanked a female Rodae, all of them smiling. "It doesn't have to be. We know how Noraddian's tied to the necromancer now."

Walter piped up. "We also have motive."

The others squinted at him in bewilderment and confusion.

Walter leaned his hip against the table's edge. "Didn't any of you have a grandfather who told you tales of travel and murder when you were growing up?"

The others shook their heads.

Walter raised the receipt in the air. "Fine, but we're still left figuring out the corundum conundrum."

Slithe rested his hand on his short sword's scabbard. "Why?"

"Why wouldn't we?"

"It doesn't concern us, does it? Are we honestly going to compute Noraddian's whereabouts relative to a grief-stricken necromancer and then arm him with two potions of invisibility?"

An idea flashed in Walter's brain and challenged his balance. "Tivara, how much do high-level spells cost to have cast for you? Like, with an enchantment."

The mage's tail quirked. "That depends, of course. Some of the trickier spells can fetch–"

Walter held up a rigid finger. "Not in silver or gold coins. How much would it cost to trade for metal bars?"

Tivara's eyes traced from side to side. "Mrrr. Anywhere from a corundum bar to a rhodium one."

Walter turned to Slithe. "You said once you're trapped in Lockspire prison, you're in for good with no hope of escape, right?"

Slithe nodded.

"Then the answer is this." Walter removed his right gauntlet and pried the copper ring of little vigor off his middle finger. He slapped it down on the pages covering the table.

Slithe glowered at him. "Get on with it."

"Right." Walter picked up the ring and held it where his party members could see it. "Enchantment. That's the solution. Follow the clues. The Rodae begged the duke to help them, and he didn't. Orantia died. Her husband, Morattidus, used his death magic to resurrect her to try to persuade the duke to safeguard their village in the future. Instead of lending assistance, the duke's guards rounded up Morattidus on trumped-up charges and shut him away in Lockspire. Now, Noraddian."

Walter clinked his ring on top of a potion bottle's cap. "Noraddian wants justice for his sister and his brother-in-law. So Noraddian decides to get his hands – er, feet? Paws? Claws? On some magic. Not that prop-up-your-other-skills-with-healing-spells stuff from the manual. He wants big, strong magic. But you can't acquire that kind of skill level overnight."

Tivara released a gentle purr. "He had the corundum infused with the magic he thought might help him break Morattidus out of Lockspire. And he paid for the corundum in rhodium bars to cover up what he was planning."

Walter almost jumped with excitement and the excess energy pumping through his body. "Yes, yes!"

Slithe spoke up. "Where's Noraddian?"

Walter slid his ring on and replaced his iron gauntlet. "Since he's not home, I surmise he got impatient waiting for the invisibility potions. With twenty-five enchanted corundum bars already in his possession, why hold out for the potions, as useful as they may be?"

Kylani's eyes burned, and her voice trembled. "There are only two problems."

Walter blinked at her. "What are they?"

"We don't know what enchantments someone armed Noraddian with. If he took off without invisibility potions, the magic he does have must be quite powerful."

Walter gulped. "That's true. What else did you think of?" His last syllable squeaked.

Kylani inspected the notice in her hands. "The charges against Morattidus aren't bogus. He raised many more dead Rodae than just his wife. He created more than fifty undead creatures. He used them as guards and protesters to intimidate the duke."

"And there's proof of this?"

"The duke saw the undead. Along with countless eye-witnesses who gave public testimony. Morattidus himself is quoted as saying he relied on the resurrected Rodae to increase his numbers to force the duke to change his policy on protecting small villages."

"My own grandfather was once misquoted in the Babbling Brook Inquirer as pronouncing his favorite breakfast was..."

Kylani held out the notice.

Walter took it and reoriented his attention. In the drawing inked onto the paper, Morattidus scowled with angled brows. Flat-eyed Rodae amassed around and behind him. Their clothes suffered numerous tears, holes, and ragged fringes. Walter stammered. "Anybody could've made this scene up from their imagination, as dark as it may be."

Kylani lunged at Walter, stopped from reaching him by the table's great expanse. A ferocious cry ripped out of her throat. "Why is it so hard for you to believe there's true evil in this world?"

Walter's mouth fell open. He tossed the disturbing notice aside and peered at the framed image of the three happy Rodae. "Because if I believe that, my quest doesn't end here. My real quest isn't to deliver two empty-looking bottles to Noraddian in the Crimson Jewel. It's to go after him and stop him from making a well-meaning mistake. We have to catch up with him and keep him from breaking Morattidus out of that prison. The necromancer might be too far gone, but we can likely talk some sense into Noraddian. If they really want protection and peace for everybody, unleashing a scary-powerful magician is no way to do it."

Silence cloaked the room.

Walter searched his friends' faces. "Right? Don't we have to do the right thing?"

Slithe chuckled in wary spurts. "Taking the ethical action might be in your purview, human. According to my code, I do what's right for Slithe." His forked tongue flitted a moment in the air.

Gruhnt eased into a polite smile. "I'll go with you, Walter." He scrunched his face into a mask of determination.

Tivara raised her paw. "Where Gruhnt goes, so do I."

Walter rested his hands on Tivara's shoulder. "Thank you both so much." He cast his eyes on the sky elf. "Kylani? Will you come?"

The elf's piercing lime-green eyes scanned the other creatures in the room. "Will it earn me more silver?"

Walter lifted his hand high in a pledge. "Kylani, I swear, I'll pay you myself from the coins I make selling what I gather from the roadside."

Kylani gave a curt bob of her head. "I'm with you."

Slithe slithered out of the room.

Walter chased him down. "Hey! In case you haven't heard right, the rest of us are going. And in case you forgot where we're going and what your specialties are, we could really use you out there."

Slithe stopped by the wooden table in the next room and whirled toward Walter. "Why would I go with you? The boy who took forever to learn the name of the city we're in now? Do you have any inkling where Lockspire is?"

Walter fired back. "No, but I can certainly ask and find out."

"Let me save you those seconds of trouble. It's in a thickly wooded area affectionately known as the Chokehold. Do you know where *that* is?"

Walter huffed. "No."

"It's in the Mossy Fold. Sound familiar? I didn't think so."

Walter rushed past Slithe to the bookshelves that hadn't collapsed to the floor under his weight. He snatched up a book and marched it up to Slithe. "*Charts and Courses through the Lovely Leaves and the Mossy Fold.* Yes, it actually did sound familiar to me."

Kylani appeared in the doorway to the secret room. "Now that we have a map, we definitely don't need him." Her eyes darted to Slithe.

Walter passed the book to Kylani. "We still might need you, Slithe. We don't know how long Noraddian's been gone. If we can't catch him before he breaks into Lockspire, we'll have to rely on your skills to get us in, too."

Slithe lowered his brows. "That seems doubtful. Wouldn't you just follow directly in his footsteps?"

"He has expensive magic he obviously shouldn't possess, or he wouldn't have gone to such great lengths to disguise it."

Kylani made a small, high sound like something being crushed. "Walter—"

The human kept his gaze locked on Slithe. "Hold on, please. Slithe, you know the territory we're heading into. That's worth as much if not more than any map in any book. If Noraddian blows the front gates open with some kind of fireball and all the guards come running, we want to sneak in past all that commotion. Don't we? Isn't that the kind of move you'd make?"

Slithe's snout twitched to one side.

Kylani pushed the open book against Walter's chest. Her words rushed out. "We don't need him, Walter. Look at the map. The route to Lockspire is self-explanatory. *A child* could get there."

Slithe's mouth slid into a lopsided grin. "I don't know about that. Even if a child could get you there, no child could sneak you in."

Walter's eyes widened. "You'll do it? You'll take us to Lockspire?"

Kylani stared at Walter. Her urgency wilted into disbelief. "No."

Walter stuck his hand out at Slithe. "Let's make it official. You'll accompany us to Lockspire and get us inside if Noraddian's already gone in. Deal?"

Slithe chuckled. "It's a deal."

Kylani shoved Walter two feet away. The book of maps clattered to the floor.

Slithe closed the distance between himself and the human. He shook Walter's hand with a dry, tight grip. "It's a done deal, sky elf."

Walter glanced at Kylani, her sudden aggression making his arms tense up.

Kylani bolted past Walter toward the door. "I'm out. I'm sorry."

Walter grabbed her forearm. "No. I just finally patched this team back together."

Kylani dragged Walter along with her, fighting to gain each new step. "We're not a *team*. Don't you get it? Do you think money magically solves everything?"

"I don't know." Walter struggled to tighten his grip on Kylani's arm.

"That's half the problem, isn't it?" Kylani jerked forward, snatching her arm free from Walter. She glowered at him over her shoulder. Her lime-green eyes speared him. "You're still learning, and you're using *us* to gain the knowledge that could one day save *your* skin. You're not the only one out there, Walter! We're not invincible just because we're higher levels than you."

Walter's mouth gaped open in silence.

Kylani reached for the door handle. "What happens if one of us gets into serious trouble? Are you going to throw a few silver coins at our attacker and hope they go away?"

Walter dove between Kylani and the wooden door. He lowered his voice. "I might be new, but I'm not stupid. You only try to opt out once Slithe joins the party."

Kylani narrowed her eyes. "If you're not stupid, why don't you realize Slithe can probably hear you? He's fifteen feet behind me."

Walter pointed to his ear. "Okay, then. Whisper it to me if you have some sort of problem with our lizard friend."

Kylani paused. She huffed and slowly leaned in close to Walter. She erupted in a shout. "I have no problem with anybody except those who ask me too many personal questions!"

Walter's ear rang so loudly, he gave up on being able to use it anytime soon. He cringed at the aching of it and flashed Kylani a thumbs-up. "Got it." Only one of his ears registered the sound of his own reply.

"Then let me past."

Walter latched his hand around the doorknob. "Wait. I was wrong, and I'm sorry."

Kylani set her foot against the bottom of the door and shoulder checked Walter away from the handle. "That's nice."

Walter's elbow popped, but his fingers stayed clamped around the doorknob. "I thought you cared about money more than anything, but you don't, do you? You care about those people. You don't want anyone else to get hurt because of Noraddian's plan to bust Morattidus out."

Kylani backed away from the door. Her eyes shimmered, and she wiped them dry with her hand.

"It's okay. It means you have a heart. It's what makes you..." Walter stopped himself before he could say the word that wasn't true.

Kylani glared at him. "I'm not *human*, human."

Walter plastered a goofy grin on his face. "I was gonna say *sky elf*."

Kylani rubbed her moist hands on her pants. "It doesn't make me anything."

"For the last time, are you in or not?" Walter held his breath.

"I'll go." Kylani sounded tired – almost defeated – but determination sharpened her eyes.

Walter exhaled his anxiety and took a deep breath of clean air. "Perfect. Thank you. And you don't need to worry so much. Tivara bought a great new blade in the marketplace. A silver dagger."

Slithe perked up across the long room. "Really? I'd like to see it if I may."

Tivara produced the weapon from beneath her cloak and handed it to Slithe. She bent down and picked up the fallen book of maps. "It's a dirk, actually."

Walter shrugged. "Whatever. They're all just knives to me, really."

The room's four other occupants gazed a thousand yards at Walter.

Gruhnt spoke up from the back of the room. "There are many different shapes of slicing weapons, Walter. It's worth learning about them if you have the time."

Slithe passed the silver dirk back to Tivara. "If you plan on ever slicing or stabbing anything again, it's helpful to know exactly what you're fighting with. You don't want to realize the differences in shape and wield after seeing what kind of hole each one opens up in you."

Walter spread his hands out from his sides. "But I don't intend to focus my skills that much."

Slithe sauntered toward Walter. "Save your groans, group. They haven't taught Walter anything so far." He gave a quick wink at Walter.

Some semblance of comfort and reassurance settled Walter's nerves. "Are we ready to go?"

Kylani brushed him away from the door. "Some of us have been ready." She pried the door open and strode into the hallway.

Walter rushed out after her. "I should go down first and get Silus out of the way. None of you are supposed to be up here."

Kylani rolled her eyes.

Tivara emerged into the corridor. "Walter's right. We all might pass through the city again on one day or another. We want to keep from making any unnecessary enemies. Go ahead, Walter. Mrow."

Walter adjusted his leather cuirass with haughty jerks and set off down the hall. "How will I signal you the all-clear?"

Tivara made a rumbling sound. "We'll be right behind you. We don't have time to lose."

Walter nodded and jogged at a furious pace down the eighteen flights of stairs to the lobby. He stumbled onto the red rug, eager to prop his hands on his knees and take a minute's rest. Instead, he popped himself upright and met Silus' amused expression.

The deskman eased into a smirk. "Sir?"

"Yes, I need your services again." Walter clenched his hands together. "I've got everything set up perfectly upstairs, but milady hasn't come home yet. I don't want anything to get ruined. Will you accompany me into the street and look for her?"

Silus swayed toward Walter, and Walter thought the deskman intended to go with him. Silus drew back again. "I'm not meant to leave my post."

Genuine irritation flared up in Walter and heated his face. He advanced a step toward Silus. "You were hired to serve the inhabitants of this building, were you not? How is my date going to feel when she arrives home to warm wine and me asleep from boredom on the couch?"

Silus walked away from the counter. "Another good point, sir."

"Come on." Walter raced to the front door and led Silus outside.

The sun had slipped further down in the sky like a lazy creature in a comfortable chair. About a dozen creatures – humans, elves, Fee'li, Cantia, and an orc – strolled the street.

Walter gestured to the left. "The last time I saw the fair elf, she was headed this way."

Silus posed a dry question. "Do you wish me to search in the opposite direction?"

"No. She must've gotten hung up talking to someone. She assured me she would return to her apartment before dark. She's probably nearby."

Walter struck off with purpose, making sure Silus kept at his side. Walter's normal hearing opened up, and he gratefully listened for the rest of his party exiting the building behind him.

A small fireball that could fit in the cup of Walter's hand sailed in an arc overhead. As soon as Walter looked up at it, it burst into a puff of black smoke. Walter glanced over his shoulder. The four other members of his party lingered outside the apartment building's doors. Gruhnt waved to him.

Walter clapped a hand on Silus' back. "I have an idea of where she might be. You keep going this way in case I'm wrong." He gave Silus a slight but encouraging push to continue on his current path.

"Whatever you want, sir."

Silus trekked on, and Walter backtracked to his group. He motioned for them to hurry out of Silus' line of sight. "Quick!" Walter hissed. "Before he sees us."

Gruhnt led the way through the shadows along the right-hand wall of close-built houses. They moved in a line for several blocks until Tivara ushered them into an arched, stone alcove leading to another garden. Its dense, wide-leaved foliage held shadows as thick as black paint.

Walter tried to keep his imagination from running wild with what he might suppose could lurk beyond their alcove. "Tivara, what's up?"

The Fee'li mage turned her paw pads up and sparked a gentle flame above them. "Who's the best at reading maps?"

Kylani raised her hand.

Tivara used her free paw to pass the book of charts and courses to the sky elf. "I'll entrust this to you, then. If we become separated for some reason, it's best to properly arm our two best navigators through the woods."

Walter's palms itched with sweat. He wiped it off on his leggings. "Separated? What happens if you, Gruhnt, and I end up apart from the two creatures who know where to go?"

Slithe sliced his clawed hand through the air in the center of the group. "Won't happen. We'd better get going. We have to cross the city to get to the right gates for the road to the Lovely Leaves."

"We're not flying out on the roc?"

Slithe shook his head. "There's no town closer to Lockspire than we already are. It's isolated for a reason, kid."

A chill crept through Walter's skin and bones. "I understand." He wished he didn't.

Tivara hid her ears under her brown hood. "Lead the way, bearded dragon." She puffed out her mystical flame.

Slithe cast a brief glance outside the alcove. He waved for the others to follow him, and they filed out into the dark street. Tivara pattered along in front of Walter. Kylani trailed right behind him with Gruhnt after her. They kept up a steady, driving pace through the paved streets.

Walter worried Slithe would steer them straight through the marketplace, where Silus was sure to be looking for Faunafloria. But they slipped past only houses, apartments, and gardens.

Even fewer other creatures straggled in the streets in the encroaching darkness. They no longer traipsed at a casual speed. They darted toward their destinations, their eyes wide as they whispered to each other in pairs and in passing.

"Did you hear about the necromancer? He's not being held very tightly. He could break out tonight and kill us all."

Someone scoffed. "That's a rumor. I read he was so powerful, the guards had to beat him half to death to bring him in."

A high, frail voice flickered. "His wife looked wretched when he brought her back from the dead. The stench was putrid."

Nausea twisted Walter's throat. He shifted uncomfortably in his armor. A quiet groan escaped him.

Tivara's ears rotated toward him under her hood. "Don't listen to them, rrrow. We'll find out the situation when we get there."

Walter swallowed and confined his focus to the back of Tivara's hood. He almost yearned for Kylani to yell in his ear again and render him deaf to the petrifying gossip.

Towering overhead, the roc's nest blocked some of the starlight. Walter recognized the building's height and took some fleeting comfort in regaining a measure of his bearings.

A familiar cackling laugh shook free from the shadows across from the nest's front door. "Is that my group of new men coming back through?"

Walter caught enough of the straw-blonde in the short mustard dress to confirm who she was. He resolved never to give her another thought.

The woman chuckled. "Half price for the tall one, eh?"

Gruhnt responded in his most pleasant of timbres. "No, thank you, ma'am. But I appreciate the attention."

Walter tried to move faster, but Slithe's and Tivara's speed kept him in check. "Hey, Slithe? Are you sure we don't need any new supplies for getting into... where we're going?"

Slithe didn't miss a beat. "Trespassing in a place like this isn't a test of supplies, lad. It's about skills, fast thinking, and silent movement."

Walter let out a humored groan at his own expense. "At least I have a decent brain, I guess."

Tivara spoke up. "You'll be fine, Walter. Mrow."

The party reached a pair of city gates and stayed on the road out into the open. Fifty feet gaped between the Crimson Jewel's protective wall and a wide expanse of woods. Walter stared at the trees. He'd never seen so many of them in his life, let alone at the same time. The roc's flight had truly taken him out of the rolling grass-topped hills of the Song Lands and plopped him down at the edge of the forested miles.

The road they walked was one of a few cutting a long, dark channel between the trees. One path ran beside a narrow track. A few wood-and-iron carts rested on the track next to a small brick building. No sound or activity made itself known to Walter from the little scene.

He pointed it out to Tivara. "Is that where the dwarves work like the guy we saw in the garden this afternoon?"

"Some of them. Others probably manage the machines in the city's foundry." Tivara angled a paw back towards the city, where black smoke billowed from a tall, cylindrical stack. "Other dwarves forge their own paths and go into another profession entirely."

"Right. I'm still thinking in stereotypes." Walter scratched his head with a twinge of irritation at himself.

"Spend more time in the world. Rrrow. The more creatures you get to know, the more you'll appreciate the diversity we have to offer."

Slithe reached the first line of trees and rapped his knuckles against one of their trunks. "Only so much moonlight can get through the leaves. If you're sure it won't catch the entire forest on fire, mage, we'd all appreciate your giving us a better light."

Tivara lifted her paw and ignited a foot-wide ball of flames. "I've never harmed anything that I didn't intend to."

The fireball floated up a foot above Slithe's head and a few feet in front of him. It flooded the party members and their dirt road with blazing illumination. On either side, Walter could see a few trees' worth into the woods. Then the trunks and leafy branches fell prey to shadow again.

Walter gulped. "Do you think there's anything – or anyone – hiding in these woods?"

Slithe led the group forward along the path. "It's always possible. It's a risk we have to take, so just stay alert."

Walter threw glances to the trees on his right and the bushes on his left. "That's my problem. I'm already on high alert."

"Maybe Tivara will let you use one of those invisibility potions." Slithe guffawed to himself.

Walter gathered his courage and what was left of his pride. "No, thank you." He looked behind him to ensure the footsteps tailing his belonged to the two unseen members of his group.

Kylani strode along as if on autopilot, her eyes dull and unfocused. Gruhnt stood almost twice her height. The slight, sleepy smile bending his lips did little to reinforce Walter's security, but the ogre-orc balanced his iron mace's thick handle over his shoulder. That shot Walter full of reassurance, and he followed in Tivara's wake much more willingly.

An owl hooted close by on Walter's left, and he jumped. "Why is my hearing under attack today?" He rubbed his throbbing ear.

Kylani responded with a smirk in her tone. "Maybe the owl found out how nosy you are."

"Wouldn't he have assaulted my nose, then?" Walter peeked back to see if Kylani smiled at his joke.

Her flat expression met him in a deadpan.

Walter hunched his shoulders up and resolved not to speak again unless someone else did.

At once, several questions popped into his head. *Are we spending the night somewhere? Are we going to use the invisibility potions if we get into trouble? How far are we walking exactly to reach Lockspire?*

Walter clamped his teeth together. He would not keep proving Slithe's and Kylani's doubts about him correct. He couldn't earn enough experience to match their levels in just a few days, but he could start conducting himself with a bit more poise.

Poise. Walter's first step out of his own house had landed him face-first in the mud. He chortled at himself, ending in a snort.

Walter straightened his posture and kept his silence. As long as he didn't draw extra attention to his lack of grace, perhaps he could get away with it.

Slithe led the party through the woods, wrapping his hand around the grip of his silver short sword. "We're about halfway through the Lovely Leaves." He jerked his head at a grey rock resting four feet tall to the left of the road.

Walter ended his vow of muteness. "Is that a landmark?"

"Yes. For those who know what it means."

Some kind of animal yowled from the shadows of the trees off to the right. A second animal screeched, and they both descended into growls.

Walter and Slithe slid their blades from their sheaths.

Metal and wood clashed dozens of times in mere seconds.

Slithe held up his short sword. "I'm going in."

Walter refused to be the last one to follow Slithe toward the unknown danger. "So am I."

"Light?"

Tivara nodded. "It's going with you."

The fireball shifted toward the animal cries. Slithe and Walter took off, dodging one tree after another. Walter pushed thinner branches aside and ducked under thicker ones.

They emerged into a tree-encased clearing. A small building like the one outside the Lovely Leaves stood here. A path and its neighboring mine cart track ran from the structure into the woods toward the Crimson Jewel.

Tivara's fireball flickered over the building's cement porch. A barrel lay on its side, and a dozen pickaxes spilled out of it onto the porch.

Two foxes scrambled together, biting and scratching. The fireball flew at them, and they took off running. They whimpered and scattered in two different directions. The fireball glided back to Walter and Slithe.

Slithe deposited his short sword in its scabbard. "Threat neutralized, if there ever was one."

Something glinted dark silver in a patch of dirt and rock by the tracks. Walter inched over to it, still on guard in case anything else living lingered in the area. He brushed some dirt aside with his boot.

Iron ore shone in the firelight, and Walter's eyes rounded in excitement. He shoved his dagger into its scabbard, missing a straight entry and having to attempt it again. He rushed over to the untidy pile of pickaxes. "Nobody minds if I borrow this, right?"

Slithe blew a breath through his nostrils. "If you're looking for ethical direction, you're asking the wrong guy."

Walter hefted a pickaxe in his hand and hurried back to the iron ore.

Slithe chuckled and folded his arms. "Afraid I might steal it?"

"Finders keepers. I need it more than you do. You have a full set of armor. Plus a silver weapon. I'm lucky to have what I have." Walter swung the pickaxe up and back over his shoulder. He brought it arcing down and broke a piece of ore loose from its moorings. "I'm also lucky mining isn't a real skill."

Slithe watched Walter free the rest of the ore. "Are you going to grab up everything you see on this whole trip?"

"As much as I can. Like I've said, I have carry weight to spare." Walter collected the four chunks of unrefined iron from the ground. "That was a pretty good deposit."

"Like I said, it adds up faster than you think. You could over-encumber yourself at a vulnerable moment. Or fill your pockets up with junk and have no room for the good stuff."

Walter tumbled the ore into his pocket and patted it. "So far, so good. And are you calling iron *junk*?" Walter hung the pickaxe off the back of his cuirass.

"Not at all. Past a certain level, a pickaxe isn't worth its weight to haul around. But you'll get there."

"Are you there?"

"Not yet. I still don't carry one as a rule."

"Why not?"

Slithe slipped into a sideways smile. "Why tip the scales with a heavy, low-cost pickaxe when many of Gladfire's highest-priced treasures weigh very little?"

Walter's eyes bulged even wider. "There's so much you can teach me."

Slithe clapped Walter on the back and guided him through the trees toward the road they were traveling. "It's all about the Rule of Ten."

"What's that?"

"The best way I've discovered to make use of how much I can shoulder. If the item's worth at least ten times its weight, nab it. If it falls short of that equation, leave it."

"What's so special about ten?"

Slithe held up his ten fingers. "Easiest math there is."

Understanding dawned on Walter. He nodded in appreciation for Slithe's simple, effective approach. "Maybe someday, I'll use that."

"Take it from me, Walter. Don't waste your time with trinkets. Don't act so desperate for money, you trade too much effort getting it."

Walter studied the Repter. More keenness shone in his golden-amber eyes than Walter had noticed before. "You live life by a lot of rules."

"It's what keeps you alive, kid."

"Will you share more of your rules with me?"

"Give it time. You can't fathom them all at once."

Walter nodded.

They stepped out of the trees and bushes onto the road. Tivara, Kylani, and Gruhnt waited for them.

The Fee'li folded one paw over the other. "What was in the woods? Mrrr."

Slithe jerked his thumb toward the mining camp in the clearing. "Couple of foxes. Your fireball maneuver scared them off."

"What took so long?"

"Walter acquired a new tool and a hobby to go with it."

Walter turned to show his pickaxe to the rest of the group.

Tivara set her mouth in a thin line. "Very nice, Walter, but we don't have time for that now. Lives might depend on us."

Walter hung his chin against his leather cuirass. "I'm sorry. I'm not used to that kind of responsibility."

"It doesn't crop up often, but when it does, I advise we all take it seriously."

Slithe started down the road. "We should keep going. The Lovely Leaves is still only the first part of our journey to Lockspire."

Walter let Tivara take her place walking behind Slithe. She directed her fireball in front of him once again. Walter followed her. He could barely hear Kylani's footfalls behind him. Gruhnt's big boots made distinctive plods.

The pickaxe jostled a little with every step Walter took. It felt like a long series of sarcastic pats on the back. *Good job picking me up, newbie. Innocent creatures might die because of you.*

Walter cleared his throat. "Should we walk faster to make up for lost time?"

Slithe called a raspy reply from the front of the line. "I don't think it makes much difference. We might have to stop to rest for a while, anyway."

"Won't it be easier to sneak into Lockspire at night?"

"Not necessarily. If we have to burn our own light, like Tivara's fireball, we risk the guards seeing it. If we try to travel only by the light of the prison's torches, we could cast shadows for them to notice."

Walter closed his eyes and attempted to store all of Slithe's departed knowledge safely away for another day. He opened his eyes again before he could bump into Tivara. "I don't have anything for sleeping outdoors. No bedroll or sleeping bag."

Kylani exhaled in annoyance. "What's the difference?"

"If you're lying outside under the stars, you want a sleeping bag. If you're taking half your belongings with you out on the road, you want a bedroll. Bedrolls are bigger and thinner."

"How come you know that but you can't tell a dagger, a dirk, and a knife apart?"

Walter set his jaw and owned his upbringing. "I grew up in a hamlet. That's why."

"Do you have some long and pointless tale about Farmer Bahooties leaving town with a bedroll?"

"Farmer Dahooti never left the hamlet. That's maybe what made him a little nuts in the first place."

Slithe flicked his forked tongue out into the air. "We're getting closer to the Mossy Fold."

Walter gladly ditched his repartee with Kylani to learn more from Slithe. "You can tell by the taste? Er, smell?"

"Yes. Different plants grow in the forest than the woods. The trees grow more densely together. Less light gets through, even in the daytime. Less fresh air, too. There's more moss. More decay."

At the thought of gathering more moss, Walter's heart leapt. "Any idea where I can buy what I need to make potions with? I always borrowed a neighbor's set back in Babbling Brook."

Slithe drew his short sword. "Kid, we make it through this mission – my apologies. Quest. I'll take you to the best alchemical shop in the Crimson Jewel personally."

Walter grimaced at the firelight flashing off Slithe's silver blade. "New, more important question. Why is your sword out?"

"The transition between the woods and the forest is an infamous chokepoint. Beasts and humanoid creatures both hide out in the thicker foliage to take travelers unaware."

Walter pulled his hunting knife out of its scabbard. "Best to be prepared, then."

A whisper-soft swipe sounded behind Walter, and he guessed Kylani had armed herself as well.

Emboldened by their previous exchange, Walter decided to have a little fun with her. "A short bow? Really? Can you use it effectively at all in such tight quarters?" Walter turned.

Kylani jabbed a narrow, three-inch bronze blade toward his abdomen. He jumped at the needle-like tip aimed at his leather cuirass and internal organs behind it.

Her eyes lit up with a light taunt. "Not so amusing when the joke's on you, is it?"

"No. What is that thing? I saw something like it back in Robin's Egg."

"It's a stiletto."

"I didn't realize you had another weapon besides your bow."

"Mine is spring-loaded. It tucks the blade inside the handle. Makes it effortless to conceal. I can keep it on me at any time."

Walter glued his wary gaze to the stiletto's sharp point. "Duly noted."

"You sure? You're not going to call it a dagger or a dirk? Or a knife?"

Slithe issued an urgent hiss through his teeth. "I heard something."

Walter faced the front of the line and left his amusements behind. He searched the illuminated sides of the road for enemies lurking amidst the trees and bushes.

An edged roar shook the leaves on their branches.

Slithe shouted. "Here they come!"

Gruhnt raced up to Slithe's side, lowering his mace from his shoulder. Tivara took up a rear position behind the rest of the group. Walter's blood pounded in his ears while his eyes waited to lock onto his next target.

With the speed and packed muscle of four dwarves rolling downhill in a single mine cart, a bear-like beast charged onto the road. Two six-inch horns protruded almost straight out from its forehead. Its eyes swirled red and green. What first appeared like thick black fur proved, in the firelight, to be bark on all of its body except its head. Thin mossy patches clung to its grooves and chips.

Slithe slashed at the horned bark bear's head. "Unless you've got a wood axe, I'd recommend aiming for what you can actually penetrate." The Repter's short sword cut into the raging beast's neck. Blood spurted a foot out.

Tivara's fireball dove at the horned bark bear's back. Other fireballs flew at the beast in a row, crashing against his bark exterior. On the fourth blast, he caught fire.

Walter rushed in, looking for a good place to strike the beast without getting injured by Gruhnt or Slithe. The horned bark bear roared again, rearing up on its back paws.

Slithe bounded to the left, away from Walter and the beast's focus. "Watch those claws!"

The horned bark bear swung a massive paw at Walter. Five enormous claws steered toward his face, and he ducked.

Gruhnt yelled out and plunged forward. He arced his mace over Walter's lowered head and connected with the beast's side. Its bark splintered, flying into Walter's hair and mouth as he tried to catch his breath.

Walter leapt up, bringing his hunting knife with him. He speared it into the beast's throat, opening a wound that spewed blood over his chin and cuirass.

Another roar erupted from behind the hurting beast. Two more horned bark bears joined the first.

Kylani sped past Walter in a blur. "I've got this one. Tivara, back me up!" She shoved her stiletto into a beast's forehead.

A quick array of fireballs darted at the beast through the narrow gap between Walter and Kylani. The blazes hit the horned bark bear, setting his back and neck on fire.

Gruhnt bellowed. "For the glory and continuation of Battle Rest!" He went after the other newly arrived foe, cracking his iron mace against its skull.

Walter and Slithe brought down the horned bark bear that had first assailed them. It thumped to the ground motionless, and Slithe broke away to aid Gruhnt. Walter turned to the other beast still grappling with Kylani.

The horned bark bear teetered on its back legs, baring ravenous teeth. Its form dwarfed the petite sky elf.

Walter tried to writhe himself between the beast and his companion. "It's three times your size!"

Kylani's eyebrows hunkered low. "You're not exactly an ogre-orc yourself, shortcake."

They rammed their blades forward at the same time. Kylani's leather glove banged against Walter's iron gauntlet and slid off.

She seethed. "Let it hit me. *Just once.* When it comes to finish me off, stab its neck. Got it?"

"Yeah." Sweat beaded on Walter's forehead.

Kylani lowered her hands, including the stiletto. The horned bark bear emitted a long groaning growl. With a great wallop, it swatted Kylani's shoulder. She cried out as the impact launched her off her feet. She landed by the road on her hip. She blinked, dazed.

The beast fell forward to balance its weight on all four paws, and Walter spent no more time observing its reaction. As the horned bark bear stepped toward Kylani, Walter lunged in, crashing to his knees. He pierced the hunting knife up through the center of the beast's lower jaw. It squealed in a bassy moan and collapsed into the dirt.

Walter's chest heaved with adrenaline. He transferred his knife to his left hand and knelt at Kylani's side. "Are you okay? Are you badly hurt?"

She shook her head. A shaky grin wobbled on her lips. "I wasn't convinced that would work."

"Some might say what I'm missing in talent, I make up for in my willingness to gain that talent." Walter stood up and offered Kylani his hand. "Do you need a healing potion? I've got one."

Kylani hesitated and pushed herself up to standing without Walter's help. She brushed grass and soil off her leather armor. "I'll feel fine after taking that rest the Repter mentioned." She snatched up her fallen stiletto.

Walter looked for Slithe. The third horned bark bear lay dead at Slithe's and Gruhnt's feet. The woods settled into an eerie peace. Walter and Slithe sheathed their blades. Gruhnt hung his shield and mace off the back of his cuirass. Kylani flicked a tiny switch on the stiletto's handle, and the needle retracted. She tucked it away in her pocket.

Tivara approached the rest of the group. "Well done, all. I'd say we've earned our rest. We'll want to be alert for Lockspire. Mrow."

Slithe nodded. "Certainly. There's a stream flowing through the forest a short walk from here. I can take us to it." He motioned to the party's armor, both leather and iron. "We're a terrible sight."

Walter examined the blood gleaming from his cuirass, gauntlets, and greaves. He spat clinging bark splinters out of his mouth. "What does it matter what we look like when we arrive at Lockspire?"

"If you get caught, it's a lot easier to make up a convincing alibi of your vulnerability if you don't show yourself to be a worthy warrior."

"Couldn't we say we were attacked and barely escaped with our lives?"

"That's the problem, lad. To survive an attack out here instantly identifies you as someone who can hold your own. We don't want the guards to have any notion of that."

The group trekked further down the road.

Walter remembered something and snapped his fingers. "In the commotion, I almost forgot." He doubled back and searched the horned bark bears for anything of value. Slithe's Rule of Ten played in his mind, but Walter didn't think that really applied here. He refused to leave behind perfectly good bark bits, fur tufts, and a few loose teeth. He collected them in his pocket and hurried to rejoin his companions.

Slithe cast a sly glance over his shoulder. "Not over-encumbered yet, eh?"

Walter smiled. "Not yet."

Slithe led the group between ever-thickening copses to a less obvious trail on the left.

Gruhnt's size snapped branches and ripped leaves as he followed the others. "Sorry, trees."

The group strolled into a long, narrow clearing along the stream's bank. The grass felt plush and cushiony under Walter's boots.

Tivara let her illuminating fireball fizzle out. "We only need moonlight here, hrow."

Slithe gave a decisive nod. "We can all take turns keeping watch if you like."

"Yes. I'd prefer to sense my enemies coming."

Kylani muttered. "Me as well. Walter and I will take the first shift."

Slithe glanced from Kylani to Walter. "Getting cozy, are you?"

Kylani took off for the bubbling stream. "Don't tell me you trust a low-level, first-time adventurer to keep a lookout on his own."

Slithe grumbled. "Good point."

Kylani removed her glove with her teeth and tested the water with her bare fingers. "We'll clean up in shifts, too. I trust Walter not to look at me." She straightened up and managed a halfway-convincing grin at Walter. "And we made a decent team taking down that horned bark bear back there."

Walter approached the stream, relieved at the chance to wash his tunic and armor. "You make a pretty good tongue twister."

Kylani clucked her tongue. "Don't ruin it, Walter."

"Right."

He watched their three companions find thick patches of grass to lie in twenty feet away. Gruhnt gave up with a shrug and plopped his massive form down, rattling the earth. A grin lit his face even as his eyes closed. Slithe settled in on his side, facing away from the stream toward the thickest gathering of trees. Tivara curled up into a ball apart from the two males. She snuggled one paw under her head and the other over her eyes.

Walter had never been this alone with Kylani. He pulled off his iron gauntlets slick with blood. "It's nice to be trusted..." He turned toward Kylani enough to find she'd already pried off her boots and leather gauntlets. He whipped his focus in the opposite direction.

"Just let me get in the water first. I don't care if you join me."

Leather and cotton rustled for half a minute. Then only the stream stirred over its dirt banks and smooth stones.

A splash of water hit Walter's cheek, shocking him with its coolness.

"Hey," Kylani called. "You cleaning up or what? We only have a few minutes until we should be on guard."

Walter left his gauntlets on the ground by Kylani's pile of clothes and armor. He peeled off his cuirass and greaves. He lifted his tunic off over his head and knelt at the stream's edge. Keeping his gaze lowered, he dipped the soiled, bloody garment into the chilly water.

Kylani spoke up so softly, Walter wasn't sure at first she was speaking at all. "It's nice to have someone around I can trust."

Walter stopped his washing. When Kylani fell silent, he resumed his task. He draped the fabric over one flat hand and rubbed his other palm over it in brisk motions.

"For battles," Kylani explained. "You know. You could've gotten scared and let that beast maul me, but you didn't. You stepped up, and you had my back. Even if it's just for this one mission –" She sighed. "–or quest or whatever, it's restored some of my faith in the people and creatures of Gladfire to know you."

Walter held up the tunic. Most of the dried mud had loosened, but no amount of water would sew up the hole from the gnome's slashing claw. He set the tunic in the grass and carried his armor to the stream. With a few handfuls of water, he rinsed the blood off. He wiped his boots clean and moved away from the stream. "I'll leave my things here to dry and start keeping watch."

"Remember to wash your face."

Walter scooped up more water and patted it over his face. "Brrr." Walking away, he shook his head as a shiver shook his spine.

The toe of his boot struck something hard. Walter squinted in the dark. Seeing nothing, he eased forward several paces. A three-inch-long bronze cylinder rested between the grass blades. *Kylani's stiletto.* Walter snatched it up. It must've fallen out of her pocket, and he'd kicked it over here. She'd want it the second she crawled out of the water.

Walter spun around to return it to her. He was about to say her name when something barely over five feet tall and pale grey puzzled him on the dirt shore. *Not something. Someone.*

Kylani stood with her back to him. Her only attire was a simple set of beige bralette and underwear. Soaking wet, they clung to her. But what drew Walter's unbelieving eyes were her limbs.

Grey-blue scars puckered along her arms like vines branching out into feathery branches.

On her legs, the scars rose as thick as ropes.

Chapter 8

A rough hand landed on Walter's arm and rocked him awake. "Naptime's over." Slithe's gruff voice penetrated Walter's grogginess. "We're getting our stuff together and heading for Lockspire soon."

Walter forced himself to nod. He'd slept, but it wouldn't have been anything he'd term *restful*.

After spotting Kylani's scars, he'd dropped her stiletto in a panic and strode toward the others. He had barely looked at her during their two-hour shift, even when she addressed him. Merely thinking about what he'd seen made a dozen more questions crop up. The biggest one reverberated through his head as Slithe ambled away.

Where the heck did scars like that come from?

Walter pushed himself up off the ground. The sun hung too low to see on account of the surrounding trees. Pink and yellow tinged the sky's hazy glow. At least the whole party had washed up by now, or so he hoped. There'd be no more unexpected nudity or inexplicable markings. He stood up and brushed off his armor.

A sharp "No!" issued from the side of the stream.

Walter snapped his attention over.

Kylani balanced on her haunches in the grass. Her eyes launched daggers up at Slithe looming over her. "I don't need your help."

Slithe hissed. "You can't find your weapon. You claim you won't leave without it. That means you need assistance."

"How about this? I don't *want* your aid." Kylani locked eyes with Walter. Her dark-purple eyebrows tilted in desperation. "Hey, Walter—"

Slithe sliced his hand through the air. "We don't need to involve the kid."

Walter strode toward Kylani. "Is this about your stiletto?"

Slithe sidestepped into Walter's path. "Take it from me. It doesn't take three party members to unearth a missing weapon.

Kylani and I were about to backtrack to where we fought the horned bark bears. The stiletto has to be somewhere between there and here."

Kylani grunted through bared teeth. "I wasn't going anywhere with you. Walter, have you seen my–"

Slithe threw his hands up. "Fine. Ask anybody. I gave you the best advice I could." He stormed off away from the stream.

Walter lowered his eyes into the grass and rubbed the back of his neck. "I did see your stiletto, actually. It should be around here by the water somewhere."

"Why didn't you give it directly to me?" Kylani hunted through the grass blades and searched around rocks.

"I wanted to, but I..." Walter licked his lips slowly. "I decided to allow you your privacy, and I assumed you'd found it yourself already. I apologize that I was wrong."

Kylani dove on her stomach to grab something and lifted her bronze stiletto out of the vegetation. She flicked the needle out and in again before she exhaled with reassurance. "You did okay, Walter. It's safe, and now so am I." She righted herself on her feet and tucked the stiletto into the sleeve of her leather armor.

"Slithe's idea was good, too. He just didn't have the information I did." Walter watched Slithe talk to Tivara for a moment. "I don't understand why he was so rude about insisting you conduct the search for it his way."

An obvious notion struck Walter upside the head, and his eyes bugged. Jealousy! Slithe had resented Walter earning Kylani's praises during the horned bark bear battle. This morning, Slithe had tried his best to get Kylani alone, perhaps to reveal he had feelings for her? And Walter had interfered, frustrating Slithe all the more.

Kylani adjusted the fit of her leather sleeve over the hidden stiletto. "Because he's an arrogant control freak?"

"Maybe he has a softer side we haven't seen before."

Slithe guffawed in Tivara's face. "I wouldn't take a chance like that in a million years!"

Kylani scoffed. "You sure about that, Walter? If he's got a soft side, I'm about to sprout wings and fly home."

Walter hazarded a glance at Kylani's face. "Where is home for you?"

She hesitated. "Let's just say it's a different kind of hamlet."

Walter grinned. "*Hamlets* I understand."

He also understood why Kylani might conceal her own softer side and shy away from those of others. With such extensive, obvious scars, committing to a romantic relationship with anyone must be challenging for her.

Slithe laughed again, more relaxed and respectful. Tivara herself chuckled, and Slithe walked away from her.

Some of Walter's tension released from his chest. "See? Slithe isn't so bad."

Kylani narrowed her eyes. "Why do you care if you convince me of this?"

Walter blinked a few times. "Sorry. I got caught up in the moment."

"What moment? Maybe you should've propped your head in the grass instead of on a rock last night."

Kylani strode away from the stream. Walter followed her and rendezvoused with the rest of the group by the trail leading out of the clearing.

Tivara lit a fresh fireball that floated in the air ahead of them. Slithe took point, and the other companions tailed him into the forest. They met up with the main road and continued deeper into the trees.

A rushing sound gradually grew into a roar. Walter peeked around Slithe and Tivara in front of him. A wood-and-rope bridge spanned a chasm in the ground. As they approached it, fear took root in Walter's belly and reached black fingers up through his stomach to his throat and tightened it. His steps slowed as if his feet were weighted. "I'm not like the rest of you. You probably got your starts earning experience and skills in unimaginably cool ways. I didn't get my first quest until I was nine. My mom charged me with finding her lost chicken. It had only wandered away behind a pile of firewood. I found it within a minute, and I earned all of five experience for it."

Staring at the bridge made Walter tremble. "What if it's forty feet down? What if I fall off this bridge, and the next thing underneath it is an iron bridge that I crash onto?"

Slithe peered over the chasm's edge. "It'd hurt. Probably knock you unconscious for a while." He pointed down into the rift. "But it'd beat screaming for a hundred feet and dying on one of those pointy rocks down there."

Walter squeaked and hung back.

Tivara swatted Slithe's arm. "It's thirty feet, Walter, rrrow. And there's plenty of water to plunge into. It'd only sting you. But they are rapids, mrow, so be careful."

Walter advanced, regaining his place in the line. Slithe and Tivara crossed the bridge ahead of him.

Tivara waved her paw to him from the other side. "Come across, Walter. It's fairly sturdy as these types of bridges go."

Walter peeked down at the racing water shooting up flying sprays off the rocks. He set his hands in wide curves around the rope railing. He took off at a sprint, determined to land on solid ground before he had another chance to freak himself out about his height.

Slithe's eyes widened. "No, Walter! Don't!"

A sharp crack split Walter's concentration, and his foot drove down through a breaking board. He yelled out, grasping at the ropes around him. His balance eluded him, and he toppled toward the bridge's floor. His knee struck the board in front of him and snapped it in two.

Walter lurched down through the square hole he'd created. He latched a hand around one of the rope balusters, and his descension stopped with a rattling jerk.

Walter wanted to look down. He didn't. He wanted to scream for help, but he didn't. He reached up and grabbed hold of another baluster on his other side. Taking a quick, deep breath, he worked at pulling himself up.

The bridge waddled a little. Slithe appeared over Walter. "It's okay. I gotcha, kid."

"Surprisingly..." Walter grunted with the effort. "I got it myself."

Slithe backed up, and Walter exerted his muscles to their limits. He raised each knee over onto the next intact board and stayed there.

Slithe applauded. "Good job. We almost lost you, but maybe you don't need us so much anymore after all."

Walter smiled. "Plus, with all that vigor I expended, I just leveled again."

Gruhnt cheered from behind Walter. "Grats, little buddy!"

"Grats," Kylani chimed in.

Tivara sounded warm with pride. "Congratulations, Walter."

Slithe beamed. "I guess hearty congratulations are in order for you, kid." He extended his hand low.

Walter took it. Emerging from the end of Slithe's sleeve poked a silver charm. Its hexagon shape wrapped around a six-pointed star. Silver filled in its center space, and a black ribbon tied it to Slithe's wrist.

The symbol all but threw Walter back onto his unknown rescuer's horse on the ride away from the gnome army. Alarms blared in Walter's head. He let go of Slithe's hand and gripped the bridge's nearest rope. His voice faltered. "Don't touch me!"

Slithe blew out a humored, disbelieving breath. "Why? What's wrong with you?"

Walter hadn't screamed when dangling through the bridge's hole, but he shouted now. "Tivara! Slithe isn't what he seems!" He didn't know what else to tell her. He didn't even know if she would believe him or act quickly enough to keep Slithe from kicking him through the bridge hole into the thunderous rapids.

A lasso of fire answered Walter's fears. It flew at Slithe from behind and wrapped itself around his back, arms, and chest. Its ends connected to form a perfect oval around him. The fire lasso nudged Slithe back to where Tivara waited. He scowled at Walter as he obeyed.

Walter pulled himself up to his feet and stalked the rest of the bridge's length. Kylani and Gruhnt joined him. Tivara led them down the path far enough that the rapids' cacophony dulled to a whisper. The fire lasso confined Slithe in place while the others banded together a few feet away from him.

Tivara lowered her hood from her head. Her golden eyes mirrored her spell's firelight. "Walter, these are serious charges."

He nodded. "I know."

"They could have serious repercussions for our gr–" Tivara corrected herself. "Party, and they certainly already do."

Slithe growled. "You're damn right."

Tivara placed the pads of her paws together. "Please explain, Walter."

Walter tossed a hand at Slithe. "He lied when I asked him if he'd been the rider on horseback who saved me from the gnomes. But that guy wore the same charm bracelet I saw on Slithe when he offered me help on the bridge."

Kylani hunched her shoulders up and locked her hands around her upper arms. "What charm?"

"A star with the middle filled in."

Kylani clamped a hand over her mouth. Her nostrils flared with each shaky breath as they came quicker and quicker. Tears rolled into her eyes. She loosened her hand a scant quarter inch. "I knew that's what you were."

Tivara screwed up her nose, and the fire lasso shrank closer around Slithe's armor. "Kylani, what do you know about this?"

Kylani shook her head. "I don't want to say."

Tivara inched closer to the sky elf. "Please do. It involves the safety of us all. It would help us decide Slithe's fate."

Kylani stepped back and pulled the stiletto out of her sleeve. She brandished it in front of Tivara and Walter. "My story is not your day's entertainment. I can still find my way back to the Crimson Jewel, and you can force this soulless Repter to guide you into whatever prison you desire."

Walter laid his gauntlet-protected hand on Kylani's shoulder. His words quivered. "Kylani, I saw them. I'm sorry."

The sky elf aimed the stiletto's point at Walter. "Saw them what? Capture me? Torture me? Barely let me escape with my life?"

Walter stared at her. "No, I saw your scars."

"Then you already know what they did." Kylani jabbed the stiletto in Slithe's direction. "What his group of repulsive exiles did to me."

Slithe lunged forward, singeing his armor against the fire lasso. He held himself still although his chest heaved. "We weren't exiled from where we came from. We left because we chose to. And you were as far away from home as we were when we found you."

Kylani shrieked at him. "Don't talk to me!"

Tivara set a paw on Kylani's arm, within inches of the stiletto's needle. "Kylani, did Slithe hurt you while you were held captive?"

"I don't think so. But they were all Repters. When Slithe insisted on traveling with us, I didn't want to take the risk that he was one of that revolting group."

Slithe chuckled. "I joined to help you. None of you are high level, or you would've been going solo instead of putting a party together. And the second time we headed out, from Noraddian's apartment? Walter begged me to go with you. I didn't even want to be here."

Kylani peered deep into Tivara's eyes. "It's a trick, Tivara. Look." The sky elf pulled out the book of charts. She opened it to a page showing a map of the larger region. "Walter asked me where my home is. It's on Sky Gouger Mountain, north of here. And as we've been traveling toward Lockspire, we've only gotten closer to where Slithe's reptilian cult kept me captive."

Slithe balked. "Ridiculous accusations."

"When I lost my weapon earlier, Slithe tried to get me alone so he could drag me back to where they imprisoned me."

"You have no proof of any of this."

Walter leaned toward Tivara. "You have to believe us. The horseback rider who saved me on the way to Hustle Hub mentioned the White Bog and Sky Gouger Mountain specifically. He had a rough voice, and he wouldn't tell me his name. He demanded to know if I'd seen anyone on my journey who didn't belong in the area."

Kylani switched her stiletto's needle inside its handle. "That's how Slithe's group thinks of sky elves, that we shouldn't stray from our mountains. It's so hypocritical. They refuse to go back to the swamps, marshes, and bogs they crawled out of."

Slithe rolled his eyes. "Lies."

Kylani peeled her sleeve back. The rising sun illuminated the network of scars on her white-grey forearm, beautiful in their shapes and terrible in meaning. "They had an electricity mage torture me with lightning for weeks."

Another detail slithered into Walter's mind, and his cheeks tensed under his eyes. "That rider called me *kid*." He strode up to Slithe as close as he could get without the fire lasso burning him. "You're the only other person or creature to call me that since I left Babbling Brook."

Slithe turned his attention to Tivara. "Are you really going to trust their words over mine? I've gone out of my way to help all of you."

Walter shook his head. "No. When I went into the inn and tavern for dinner two days ago, it was crowded with suspicious characters. Including somebody in a red cloak. I got so wound up about the Fox Thief and joining the party, I forgot all about that cloak. But it was the same color as Slithe's."

Walter backed away from the Repter. His lip curled. "Slithe sat there on that bench and heard everything we talked about. Once Kylani came in and expressed interest in helping us on our quest, Slithe offered his services."

Slithe diverted his gaze to the path ahead. "Nonsense."

Tivara's paw drew a circle in the air, forming a new fire lasso around the base of Slithe's tail. "No more words out of you until Kylani's been heard out. This would never grow back if I recall my lessons on Gladfire's race varieties correctly."

Slithe clenched his teeth, doubling the bulging tension in his jaw.

Kylani rolled her sleeve down over her scarred arm and stuck the stiletto back inside the sleeve's end. "There were too many personal complications entwining on Sky Gouger. Especially in Snowcrest, my village. I left so I could do my own thing in my own way. No one off the mountain would have any knowledge of my past and judge me by it."

She stabbed Slithe with a glower. "Then a group of Repters captured me. I was minding my own business between towns, and they knocked me out. When I came to, I didn't know where I was. Some sort of mud-and-clay building. Only I wasn't a guest with run of the place. They confined me in manacles to the floor of one room. The door was made of iron bars, so I could see the Repters passing by in the hallway. I could hear screams and pleading of other prisoners like me."

Walter's mouth hung open. He fumbled at sweeping his hair off his forehead. "How did you get out?"

"Trying to rush the story?" Kylani granted Walter the ghost of a forgiving smirk. "I don't know exactly how long I was there. The Repters who came in told me I didn't belong off the mountain. They said if I promised to go home and they saw that I went that way, they'd let me go. I wanted to wander free instead, so they sent in a Repter with electricity magic. He shocked my arms and legs one at a time. The lightning was so intense, I shook uncontrollably until I blacked out."

Kylani tugged her sleeve ends further down over her wrists. "They didn't care how much I cried. Except one. He said he'd unlock the manacles and let me go."

Tivara tilted her head to one side. "Did he say why?"

"He knew what they were doing was wrong. He didn't want to be alone by leaving the group, but he couldn't go home, either. Some of the other captives had acted against Repters or Gladfire, so he didn't feel as sorry for them. But I was just a traveler, almost the same as him. He kept the rest of the Repters busy while the other captives slept, and I snuck out."

"How long ago was this?"

"A few months. I've been looking over my shoulder and watching my back ever since. The chance was too high that one or more of those Repters would come to take me back there. And I can't go back. To the Repters or Sky Gouger."

Tivara turned to Slithe. "At the risk of losing your tail, your sense of balance, and your ability to live an athletic life in this world, I suggest you tell the truth."

The smaller fire lasso glowed more brightly around the Repter's tail.

Slithe twitched. "You wouldn't dare, and you know it. I could trim your tail off before you'd sever mine."

Gruhnt stomped up to Slithe and drew his gigantic mace. He growled in Slithe's face. "Speak, lizard, or you'll dream of forty-foot drops as I cream you into the ground."

Kylani produced her short bow and armed it with an iron-tipped arrow aimed at Slithe's nose.

Slithe showed his teeth in an uncomfortable grimace. "All right."

Walter pointed to the grass. "Start from the beginning. Or explain where the beginning was?"

Tivara stood up straighter. Her ears rotated toward their hostage. "What is your group, Repter?"

Slithe rubbed his fingertips over the charm bound to his wrist. "The Isolated Six. We saw no great harm in occasional banditry, but our community disagreed. They wished us to stop targeting even the most greedy, unethical traders, shopkeepers, and artisans. In the end, it's hard to say whether we left by choice or were forced out."

"And why did you capture others like Kylani?"

Slithe sneered. "Because no creature should leave their home. By exile or by determination. Whether our new communities accept us or reject us. We should be home, where we were born, where we're meant to be."

Walter ground his teeth together. "That includes me, doesn't it? I traveled away from the hamlet."

Slithe snarled. "But nobody would know that, would they, if you didn't constantly advertise it?"

"I don't understand. Do you have a problem with me or not?"

"I didn't have to, but you prove my point more and more every day. You don't belong out here, boy. You were made for hamlet life, not traveling between towns and major cities."

Walter spun away and crossed his arms.

Slithe sputtered behind him. "That's just the way it goes. It's not personal. You don't have the stamina, the strength, or the cunning to survive out here. Just like Kylani and the other sky elves are best suited to survive in the snow. And Repters thrive in marshes, swamps, and bogs."

Walter blew a raspberry. His tone slid into sarcasm. "What about orcs and ogres? And cat-people?"

Slithe's timbre smoothed over. "Come on, Walter. Can you really picture Tivara slogging through the White Bog and loving it? Do you want tall, muscular orcs and ogres moving to the deserts where they couldn't even find the foods or materials they're used to?"

Walter faced Slithe and lined himself up at Kylani's side. "I want the same thing I imagine Kylani wants. For all of us to have the freedoms we choose."

Slithe rolled his eyes. "That figures. One day, you'll find out the Isolated Six are right. Maybe you'll learn the hard way. Maybe you'll get off easy."

Tivara curled her paw into a fist, and the two fire lassos encroached on Slithe a little more. "So you joined our group to kidnap Kylani? Is that it?"

Slithe pressed his arms against his sides and nodded. "She shouldn't be down here. And she's already caused our group extra trouble by turning one of us traitorous and costing me so much time and effort to track her down."

Kylani narrowed her eyes and reset the arrow against her bowstring. "I turned no one, kidnapper."

Walter tossed his hands up. "Was the Fox Thief half as bad as you told us he was?"

Slithe shrugged. "I have no idea."

Tivara waved at Kylani's bow. "Put it away, elf. I've made my decisions for the day. Repter, you are to remain without your freedom within the confines of my fire magic. You will do as you already promised and use your skills to help us enter Lockspire as necessary. Rrrow? Because there's one other creature's freedom even more detrimental to our own, and that's Morattidus'."

Kylani put her bow and arrow away with a begrudging purse of her lips.

Walter moved to continue following the road through the forest. "That's right. Mo and No."

His companions' four sets of eyes fixed themselves on him.

Tivara slapped a paw over her face.

Slithe chuckled. "Did you seriously just reduce a deadly necromancer and his co-conspirator to one-syllable nicknames? And the rest of you have *me* restrained in magic. He's the one who's a danger to you."

Tivara walked away toward their destination. "Come. We'd best get moving. You've wasted enough of our time and energy, Slithe."

The fire lassos floated after Tivara, and Slithe hurried to realign himself within their circles.

Walter's shoulders hunched over, his chest smoldering at Slithe's remarks. "All of this is your fault, Slithe. You did everything you could to trick and manipulate us."

Slithe flicked his forked tongue in the air. "Sorry, kid. You just make it too easy. All I had to do in that apartment back there was act like I didn't want to help you anymore. You invited me along and practically rolled out the red carpet for me to accompany you."

Walter shoved his hands in his pockets. "Why couldn't you just have a crush on Kylani like I thought you did? Everything would be simpler."

Slithe choked. "Maybe for you. Repters and sky elves don't mix, kid."

Kylani speared Walter's shoulder blade with the tip of her finger from behind. "Hey. This guy's a kidnapper, not an admirer. Don't be gross."

Walter kicked at pebbles along the dirt road. "In my own defense, Kylani's a really cool elf once you get to know her better. And Slithe, well, he's got a lot of wisdom from his travels."

Slithe tossed back a "thanks" from in front of Walter.

The human scrunched his nose up. "Hey, Slithe? Do me one favor?"

"Sure, kid."

"Don't ever *grats* me again. I don't want anything more from you."

"I meant what I said."

Walter talked past a lump in his throat. "I didn't say you couldn't mean it. I just want you not to say it."

Chapter 9

All around Walter, his companions groaned and grunted. Walter himself let out some kind of a tense squeal.

The forest had thickened, pitting close-standing trees against each other for sunlight at the top of the canopy. Meanwhile, down on the ground, Walter and his fellow travelers worked hard to squeeze themselves through any sizable gaps in the foliage. Ferns tripped them. Vines ensnared their ankles and boot treads.

Walter dangled three feet off the ground, his waist caught in the V between two trunks angling from the same tree base. "Tivara, help me!"

Halfway up the oak ahead of Walter, Tivara looked down with pity in her glossy eyes. "You can use my tail for leverage, Walter, but don't pull on it. Mrow?"

Tivara lowered her grey-and-black tail in front of Walter. He grabbed hold of it with both hands and wiggled forward. Tivara yowled as he surged free from his confines. Walter found his footing on the dry earth, and Tivara raised her tail to lick its wrenched fur.

Gruhnt cried out in despair. "How did you get through, Walter?"

Walter studied the jungle gym of a path he'd crawled through the last twenty feet. "I barely made it to where I am, big guy. I think you're gonna have to break some more tree limbs to follow us."

Gruhnt cracked his mace against a thick branch, splitting it from the trunk. "Sorry." He advanced a step and walloped an oak limb with his mace. It crashed to the ground. "Sorry."

Walter peered through the leaves to his right. "Kylani? You still with us?"

Camouflaged, the sky elf huffed with effort. A moment later, her boots landed with a clap against wood. A few green leaves floated down to the forest floor.

Walter set his hands on his hips. "That's a yes."

Slithe hummed somewhere up ahead. "Enjoying your trek through the Chokehold yet?"

Tivara rumbled with a low growl. "I agree with Walter. It's better if you keep your mouth shut, Slithe."

"It'd be a lot easier for me to lead you through this part of the forest if you'd at least loosen these fire rings."

Tivara pounced down to the ground. "Loosen? Prow! I was thinking about tightening them again "

Slithe's timbre relaxed. "You'll widen them soon, anyway."

Walter bunched his eyebrows up. "Why would you think that, you cocky kidnapper?"

"Because we're almost there."

Only dimly lit trees, feathery ferns, errant stalks of grass, and winding vines surrounded Walter. "The parade of lies continues."

A soft cough sounded from high in the trees. Kylani called down. "No, he's right. I can see the prison."

A slam right behind Walter sent another massive tree limb thundering to the ground. Gruhnt arrived next to Walter and rested his mace handle over his shoulder.

Tivara looked up toward Kylani's position. "Do you see any Rodae?"

"No."

"What about entrances?"

"There's a wall with guard towers. Beyond that, there are a few small doors far apart from each other."

Slithe let out an impatient breath through his nostrils. "I could've told you that, cat. I led us directly to the side of the place. We have the best chance of going in through one of these entrances."

Tivara met Slithe's gaze. "Do you know for sure exactly which one?"

"Of course."

"Do you mind telling us?"

"I swore to take you inside. Why would I disadvantage myself now by giving over one of my most valuable secrets?"

Tivara frowned. "I understand. Well, with no signs of Noraddian, we have no choice but to infiltrate the prison."

Slithe tilted his head. "You're forgetting one important fact."

"Brrow?"

"We have to infiltrate the grounds first. That's every bit as tricky."

Kylani rustled amidst the leaves. "You're forgetting I learned an important lesson on sneaking when I escaped your capture. Create a diversion. That night, it was stories of home cooking and overblown fantasies of Equiconian female dancers."

Slithe balked. "I knew those purported exploits were fake."

A brief noise like a hollow, sliding whisper issued from Kylani's spot amongst the tree branches.

Seconds afterward, screaming erupted beyond the forest's stranglehold.

Slithe hissed up at Kylani. "What did you do?"

Kylani climbed down from one limb to another and landed on her feet. She smirked at Slithe. "I shot one of the guards with my arrow."

Slithe flapped his mouth in silence before his voice found traction. "You idiot. You've alerted them to our presence."

Kylani folded her arms. "*A* presence. Not ours."

"They'll be looking for someone."

"And tending to their dead or dying friend." Kylani opened her eyes wide in false astonishment. "I hope I didn't kill a guard and create a commotion right in front of the very door you planned to lead us through."

Slithe's shoulder twitched toward Kylani, but he held himself in check before the fire lassos could cut into him. "You fool. You're playing games at a time like this?"

Kylani inspected the Repter's face. "You're looking quite pale. What's the matter? Don't want to get captured this close to Lockspire?"

Slithe writhed. With a crackling sound, the fire lasso flared up around his torso and singed a line in his leather armor below his right shoulder. He constricted himself within the magic's confines. "How dare you? All of you?"

Gruhnt hefted his mace down from its perch atop his own shoulder and slapped it several times into his opposite palm. He grimaced at Slithe.

The Repter's eyes darted ahead. "Okay. But we're out of time now. We have to clear the Chokehold and find a place to hide against the outer wall."

Gruhnt raised his mace.

Walter cringed. "Quietly, buddy."

Gruhnt bared his teeth in embarrassment. He tucked his mace away and ripped the nearest tree limb free with his bare hands in one smooth motion. The wood popped, and Gruhnt set it gently on the ground.

Walter gave him a thumbs-up. "Can you make a path for all of us?"

Gruhnt tore a low-hanging branch off the next maple.

A realization slapped Walter in the face. "Wait. Why didn't we have Gruhnt clear a path for us to get here?"

Tivara kept her voice low. "Because he can't hide as well as we can. We needed to go first."

Slithe spoke up again. "Right now, we need to get out of these trees. The guards will come looking for whoever shot that arrow any minute."

Kylani grinned at him, a mix of daring and self-satisfaction. She pulled her short bow off her back and slipped an arrow from its quiver.

Gruhnt parted more tree limbs from their trunks until he broke through into the full light of the day. Kylani rushed through the hole, and Walter ran out after her. Tivara, Slithe, and Gruhnt trailed after them.

A guard tower stood twelve feet in front of them. Two cloaked creatures manned it. Beyond the wall, Lockspire prison jutted up twenty stories against the grey sky. The right side of its tower only rose half that height, leaving a jagged stone pinnacle the rest of the way. The building's black blocks formed a random pattern of matte stone and glossy volcanic matter.

The group sprinted ahead and flattened their backs against the black stone wall. Tivara waved her paw, and the fire lasso hovering around Slithe's torso dissipated.

Walter threw a glance to his right. A glint of metal nabbed his attention, and he studied it more closely. *Iron.* He set the tip of his tongue between his lips and sidled along the wall toward the ore deposit sparkling in a mound of red clay. Walter unhooked his pickaxe from the back of his leather cuirass.

"Psst!"

Walter looked over his shoulder.

Kylani stared at him. "Are you kidding? You'll get us caught making that kind of racket."

"Would you believe me if I said it was meant to be a distraction for the guards?"

Kylani's nostrils flared.

"I didn't think so." Walter brought the pickaxe's tip down onto the ore. With three hearty swings, he managed to split the ore free. He put up his pickaxe and gathered the ore into his pocket.

"Don't forget the clay, Einstein."

"Oh, right." Walter picked up a handful of moist clay.

A density Walter had never experienced before nearly bolted him in place and limited his movements. "Aw, crap."

Kylani eyed him. "What?"

"I think I'm over-encumbered. I can barely walk over to you." Walter tried to take a normal step but struggled to cross half the distance.

Kylani reached out. "Give me the clay."

Walter fought to take a second half-step.

Kylani wiggled her fingers. "Hurry up. I'll give it right back to you after we stop Noraddian."

Walter sighed. He passed the clay to Kylani. His invisible chains lifted.

Kylani stored the clay in her pocket. "Hey, I have an idea. Let me see your pickaxe for a second."

Walter handed it over.

Kylani stepped away from the wall and chucked the pickaxe as hard as she could into the forest. It sliced through leaves and banged against a wide tree trunk.

Walter's mouth popped open in protest, but Kylani clamped a hand over it.

A deep voice called out from the guard's tower above the group. "Definitely noise and movement over here."

Kylani pointed past Walter. "*That's* how you use your pickaxe for a distraction. Go!"

Walter scurried along the wall past the remaining clay on the ground. Kylani motioned to Gruhnt to link his fingers together, and he formed a step up with his big hands. Kylani used it to vault up and over the wall. Gruhnt turned to Walter, and the human wasted no time by questioning Kylani's plan. He set a boot in Gruhnt's hands and jumped over the wall. He landed on his feet beside Kylani and thanked his lucky stars not to have planted in the mud.

Tivara and Slithe sprang down next to him. Gruhnt hoisted himself up and over.

Several large wagons sat vacant in the yard. Storage barrels occupied the corners of the wall's perimeter. Taller wagons equipped with holding cells and iron-barred windows stood on the far side of the grounds.

Slithe jerked his chin at them. "Those are pretty close to the main entrance."

Walter scratched his arm through his sleeve. "What do we do now?"

The Repter tasted the still air. "We make a break for the middle door over there to the left. Be as quiet as you can. For now, the guards aren't looking for us in any of the right places." Slithe crept away from the outer wall.

A soft tap of wood against wood made Kylani's eyes grow wide. "Yes, they are. Get down!"

Kylani jumped at Slithe. An arrow pierced the air as she tackled him to the ground. The arrow lodged in Kylani's shoulder, and she gasped in shock.

Walter raced to her side and knelt down. "Are you okay?"

Kylani gritted her teeth. She steadied the arrow with her hand. "Peachy."

Tivara waved toward the nearest wagon. "We should get to cover."

Walter offered Kylani extra support as she pushed herself up. She leaned on his arm, and the five of them scrambled to the safety of the wagon's long side. Gruhnt curled up into the smallest ball he could.

Walter searched Tivara's face. "What do we do? How do we fix Kylani's injury?"

Tivara hesitated.

Kylani cleared her throat. "She doesn't want to tell you, Walter. There's only one quick way to deal with this considering the skill set we've got."

Walter firmed up his resolution. "What can I do?"

Kylani nodded to Tivara. "Don't throw up."

"Why would I do that?"

Tivara poised her paw over the offending arrow tip. Kylani bit her lip and yanked the arrow out. Blood only had a moment to drip from the wound before Tivara blasted it with a small dose of fire. Kylani thudded her boot heels against the ground. The stench of burning leather and flesh filled Walter's nose. He made a preemptive swallow and turned his gaze away.

After several seconds, he dared to peek at Kylani.

Sweat beaded on her white-grey forehead. She granted him a weak, woozy smile. "That's why. Cauterizing it takes quick magic. Patching me up would take time and bandages we don't have."

Walter showed her the green health potion from his pocket. "I still have this."

"Save it. We're not even inside yet."

Tivara shifted her whiskers. "And the guards might be closing in. Slithe?"

The Repter sat behind Kylani with his back slumped against the wagon. He shook his head slowly, his eyes trained on the ground.

Tivara patted her paws together by his face. "Slithe. Come on. The door might be locked. There could be traps set up inside."

Slithe murmured. "You owed me nothing."

Tivara smacked Slithe's leg. "We don't have time for babbling."

Walter jabbed his thumb against his chest. "And I should know. I come from Babbling Brook."

Slithe gawked at Kylani. "Why did you do it?"

Kylani scoffed. "Don't get a conscience now."

"But if you knew... if you really knew what it was like. Why we were doing it..." Slithe laid his hands over the pointed scales framing his face. "We can't go back home. Ever. And you and so many other creatures willingly gave up your homes. It outraged us to the point where we went mad."

Tivara's features softened. "The Isolated Six?"

"Yes. We wanted to punish you. To show you the error of your decision. To steer you back to the homes that would actually have you."

Kylani spat at Slithe. "Screw you. You have no idea what mess I fled from in Snowcrest."

Slithe's tired eyes glittered with wetness. "But you weren't forced out. You weren't exiled and told to die as far from home as possible."

Kylani stiffened. "No, I wasn't. I left before that could happen."

"So you showed good judgment where the Isolated Six and I didn't, at home and where we imprisoned you. I'm so sorry we subjected you to those shocks, Kylani." He reached out to her.

She scooted back. "It's not that easy, lizard. I hope you die close enough to the mountains that Chorda feast on your skin and your insides."

Walter hung his head in defeat. "I don't know what Chorda are. You lost me back at Equiconian."

Kylani's green eyes flashed. "Chorda are owl-people. Some of them live on Sky Gouger."

"We'll settle the rest of my ignorance later." Walter laid his hand on Kylani's healthy shoulder. "I know none of us want to accept an apology from Slithe at the moment, but maybe you should hear him out. He did save my life from the angry gnomes. He didn't have to do that. He might've been rude and dodgy, but I escaped that skirmish with only a scratch thanks to his generosity."

"Then you hug it out with Slithe. I'm through with him."

Slithe extended his hand toward Kylani again. "I should've never hunted you down. I should've been happy you got out. Our resentments blinded us. Please. Consider yourself free now. I'll hunt you no more."

Kylani rose to her haunches. "I only saved you so we could rescue Gladfire from Morattidus."

"I know."

"Will you let your other prisoners go?"

"Naturally. I–"

An arrow whistled past Kylani's injured shoulder. The silver tip sailed through Slithe's neck and emerged a few inches out the other side. Blood streamed from both wounds. Slithe gurgled as he tried to inhale. The blood pouring from his neck filled with bubbles that popped.

Gruhnt shimmied away from the arrow that had come to rest less than a foot from his face.

Kylani spun on her feet and equipped her bow. She loaded an arrow in the time it took Walter to blink. Kylani let it fly at a guard who had circled around the wagon. Her arrow capitalized on a gap in his helmet, sticking in his forehead and dropping him to the ground.

Walter's mind churned as he leaned over Slithe with Tivara. "You got any magic for this? Can we save him?"

Tivara fell quiet. "No, Walter. I don't think so."

Kylani leapt up to her full height. "We got more company." She readied and fired three more arrows in rapid succession at opponents Walter couldn't see.

Tivara piped up. "How many?"

"A dozen at least."

Tivara patted Gruhnt's knee. "Back over the wall. Help us, Gruhnt."

Kylani's arrows held the advancing guards back as Gruhnt rolled up to his feet. Tivara shot several small fire blasts at various armored foe. Walter tugged on Slithe's leather sleeve. The Repter's eyes stared off without focusing, his body limp and motionless against the wagon.

Gruhnt ran for the outer wall. "Come on, little buddy."

Walter's eyes watered as he studied Slithe's face. "We can't just... leave him."

Tivara backed up toward the wall where Gruhnt waited for them. "Yes, we can. Mrow. It's not the best situation, I'll grant you that. But we can't squander time with sentimentality while we're under fire."

Walter nodded. He drew the enchanted hunting knife Slithe had given him. In double time, Walter sliced through the black ribbon bracelet tied around Slithe's wrist. Walter tucked it in his pocket and ambled toward Gruhnt. Kylani and Tivara rushed past him, trading additional volleys with the guards as they moved.

Gruhnt hoisted Tivara over the top of the wall.

Kylani sent another arrow flying, knocking the nearest guard down on one knee. "Go, Walter!"

Walter hesitated, agonizing over Slithe's lifeless body left behind.

Kylani grunted in aggravation. She climbed up into Gruhnt's linked hands and disappeared over the wall. Gruhnt pulled himself up and sat straddling the wall's apex. He reached a hand down to Walter.

Walter gulped. "Goodbye, old friend." He grabbed Gruhnt's hand, and the ogre-orc lifted him up to the top of the wall.

The two companions dropped down to their feet in unison.

Kylani held onto her short bow in one hand and shoved Walter with her free palm. "What the hell was that? You could've gotten us killed, and that sack of scaly shit wasn't worth it."

Walter scowled. "Maybe you don't get to decide who's worth crying over and who's not. Slithe may have joined our party with bad intentions, but he taught me valuable lessons. And in the end, you wouldn't even let him take an arrow if you could help it. You changed his mind about what he and the rest of the Six were doing."

"A lot of good that does. He promised to free their prisoners, and he died before he could do so much as mention it to the group."

Walter showed her the bracelet, its silver charm dangling. "I took proof that we knew Slithe."

"It doesn't solve anything."

"But it's something, isn't it?"

Kylani's gaze raked him, conflicted between humor and ire. "We haven't gotten ourselves out of our current mess, and you want to go up against magicians and torturers?"

"Yes, I do."

Tivara's paw tapped Walter's shoulder. "Kylani has a point, Walter. Rrrow. One mission at a time. We've lost Slithe's skill set to get us inside. We don't even have his tools to fumble our way through this place on our own."

Walter buried Slithe's bracelet deep in his pocket. "Any ideas?"

Rustling leaves snatched the four companions' attention to the dense forest twelve feet away. Branches shook, and green leaves danced.

Kylani drew an arrow. "I have an idea. Prepare for battle."

Chapter 10

Walter brandished his hunting knife He fought to keep his resolve steely. Could he attack a guard who was simply doing his job? Could he *kill* a guard if it came down to it?

Gruhnt chuckled low in his throat. He thumped his mace handle against his open palm.

Kylani stood like a marble statue, arrow perched against her bowstring. Tivara held her paws up toward the unseen creature or beast who approached.

Walter couldn't decide between asking for more advice from his group and issuing a threat to their would-be assailant.

A twig snapped. Walter pivoted to his left.

Six feet to the right, a shadowy ball rolled through the air out of the forest. It sprang open before it reached the grass, revealing four tiny paws and a black nose on a white snout. With the flick of a paw, the nearly-invisible creature flipped down the hood of its robe.

The Fox Thief regarded the party with his amber eyes. He vacillated his whiskers from side to side.

Walter's rigid stance deflated, and he lowered his knife. "We nearly killed you!"

The Fox Thief squeaked. "My demise wasn't as imminent as that."

"What are you doing here? The last time we saw you was three towns ago. And you turned us down when we asked for your help."

The Fox Thief placed his palms together and bowed his head over them. "My apologies. I had a quest of my own."

Walter raised his index finger. "See? He called it a *quest*. Which you didn't a minute ago, Tivara."

The Fox Thief strutted closer. "Albeit, my journey was less altruistic than yours."

"Why tell us anything now?"

"I'm glad I caught up with you. It was your party who ransacked the Rodae's apartment in the Crimson Jewel, was it not?"

Walter gaped at the Vulyon. "Yeah. How did you know?"

The Fox Thief considered Walter's arms. "I thumb and arm wrestled you back in Hustle Hub. When I discovered the Golden Silks apartment in complete disarray with its secret room not-so-secretly ajar, I assumed only one newbie human could've been responsible."

Walter ruffled his hand through his hair. "I may have knocked over a few things. What brought you to Noraddian's apartment?"

The Vulyon squinted. "I thought the reason was clearly inherent by my name. I'm a thief by trade, and rumors reached my ears that highly specialized, expensive goods had recently been sold to the owner of that apartment. Noraddian, you say?"

"Yes." Walter's shoulders slumped anew. "You're probably here to steal the magic corundum right from him?"

"Don't leap to too many conclusions, young human. I came to turn a profit, yes, but mainly to offer my services. With the secret room wide open, I did some quick reading. I surmised you came to Lockspire to thwart Noraddian's plan to help his village by freeing the necromancer." The Fox Thief pointed to the top of the black tower.

"That's right. And we just lost our friend, the thief we hired to get us inside." Walter shot a glance at Kylani, but she offered only a blank expression.

The Fox Thief draped his hood over his head in one swift motion. "Have you seen or heard Noraddian at all?"

"No. We think he's already inside."

"Then we're already out of time. If you agree to pay me for my aid, whatever amount you can, I'll lead you in until we meet with Noraddian."

Walter nodded. "Anything. We have to stop him."

"The corundum is mine."

"Of course."

"Follow me."

The Fox Thief took off, most of him impossible to make out against the grass and the wall. Only his four paws stuck out of his enchanted cloak. Walter and his three companions rushed off after the diminutive Vulyon.

Walter cleared his throat. "Um, wouldn't it be easier for us to follow you if you left your hood down?"

The Fox Thief's small, gently husky voice floated from thin air. "The guards would see me. No sense in that."

"Okay. Second question. Do you want Gruhnt to boost us up over the wall again?"

"Ha ha! Silly notion. Didn't anyone tell you I'm the best thief in all of Gladfire?"

"I believe the waitress said *one of the best*. Are you a bit prideful, fox?"

"Prideful or honest?" The shadowy figure stopped, and its tiny paw flourished at a part of the wall. With a push against one of the stones, a section six-feet square swung open like a door.

Walter's eyes popped wide. "Holy mackerel! Slithe didn't know about this, or he'd have led us over this way."

The Fox Thief brushed his paws against each other, satisfied. "Honest it is, then. Come. Quickly."

Walter followed the shadowy figure through the doorway in the wall. Tivara and Kylani stayed close on his heels. Gruhnt lowered himself to his hands and knees to crawl through after them.

The Fox Thief waved for them to keep up with him. He raced straight to a door in the prison and produced a pair of lockpicks. He worked them in the lock with deft, precise movements.

Walter couldn't understand what the Fox Thief looked, listened, or felt for. "How do you know this door is locked?"

"It always is, unless they're using it. Did you think an entrance directly inside a hidden doorway would be left accessible?"

The latch clicked, and the Fox Thief secured his tools. Walter remained silent. Any intelligent answer eluded him.

The Fox Thief inched the door open. "Be ready."

"To hide? Fight?"

"Whatever the event requires. Here we go."

Walter engaged his leg muscles to cross the threshold into Lockspire prison. His foot remained stuck to the ground. *Over-encumbered at a time like this!* But he hadn't picked up so much as a leaf or an insect's wing since he unearthed the iron ore and clay.

He directed his gaze up over two hundred feet to the top of Lockspire's black pinnacle. *I don't need to lower my carry weight. I just have to increase my courage.*

With a deep, invigorating breath, Walter charged in behind the Fox Thief's shadowy outline. The rest of his party trekked in after them.

Walter kept his hunting knife at the ready. "I want all of you to know how much I appreciate your mastery in the skills you've chosen."

Kylani hissed at him. "Hush!"

Tivara whispered right behind him. "Thank you, Walter. We know."

Walter glanced around the small room. Sunlight streamed in from two small, high rectangular windows flanking the entrance. Storage barrels and chests built of hard woods filled the right-hand wall. Empty tables sat to the left.

The urge mounted in Walter to pry into the nature of the room and why that's where the secret door led. He willed himself to keep silent.

The Fox Thief reached the door at the other end of the room. He pulled out his lockpicks and stopped halfway to their intended aperture.

Walter gave up his concentration. "What's wrong?"

"It must be trapped. Otherwise, it's too easy." The Fox Thief held the lockpicks between his lips. He felt along the crack between the door and its frame. "Yes. A thin thread here."

"Can you pull it out?"

The Fox Thief dropped his lockpicks into one paw. His voice strained high and quiet. "Pull it? Never pull on *anything*, boy! Is that understood?"

"Yes, sir."

The Vulyon thief produced a shiny pair of silver scissors. He snipped where Walter could see nothing of note and deposited the scissors inside his enchanted cloak.

Walter pointed to the place where the Fox Thief had delivered his snip. "How do we know you cut anything?"

"I'll ring your neck with the thread. Do you accept that as proof enough?" The Fox Thief inserted his thin metal tools into the lock.

Walter rubbed the back of his neck. "Man, it's almost like having Slithe with us again."

The Fox Thief's employment of the picks elicited another click, and he moved up against the door. "Cat mage, might I request your assistance? I detect no guards in this hallway. I do hear several voices off to the left."

Tivara sidled up to the doorjamb. "That's what I hear, too."

"See, human? I'm fully capable of manners when it suits me. Here we go."

The door swung inward, and Walter rolled his eyes. The group darted off to the left. Three small levers stuck out of the wall outside the storage room.

The Fox Thief patted one as he whisked past them. "These likely allow the guards to bypass the trap if they know the correct code to enter."

Three rough voices wove together up ahead.

Walter whispered to the Fox Thief. "Wrong way?"

The shadowy form shook its head. "Guards stay behind to protect the records. We need to know where the necromancer's being kept."

"If you don't want to bother with their whole, long names, I came up with some pretty good nicknames for the two Rodae we're after."

"No!"

"Okay. I also play a very convincing, mean-spirited rich guy if you want a solid diversion."

"Actually, human, I do."

The Fox Thief's paw shot out and snatched Walter's wrist. The Vulyon slung Walter forward down the hall. Walter teetered off balance, pitching to all sides. He finally righted himself and turned to reprimand the thief.

Instead, three gruff voices barked in alarm and interrupted Walter's plans.

Walter had found his equilibrium directly in front of an open doorway. Inside the room, one guard sat at a bulky metal desk. Two others stood over him. They advanced toward the doorway, drawing their swords.

"You can't be here!" one guard bellowed.

"How did you get in?" another demanded.

Walter plastered a wavering grin on his face and raised his palms in surrender. "Would you believe I'm looking for Faunafloria? Statuesque darling of a moss elf."

Walter reeled backward as the three guards emerged into the hallway, glowering under bushy eyebrows.

A tiny paw threw something at the stone floor, and smoke exploded around the guards. They squinched their eyes shut and choked on the grey clouds.

"Hurry!" the Fox Thief suggested.

Walter and his companions covered their noses and mouths as they scurried into the office.

The Fox Thief jumped up on the desk and tore open a book of records resting on it. "What did you say this necromancer's name was?"

Walter almost made a joke but delivered the full name. "Morattidus."

The thief flipped through a few pages before he ripped one out. "The spire. The necromancer's jailed all the way at the top."

Walter moaned. "More stairs?"

The Fox Thief chortled. "Never visited the Sandstone Pillar, did you?"

"I don't think so."

"Never climbed up or down a mountain like your sky elf companion, eh?"

Kylani snorted. "I should say not."

The Fox Thief folded the record page and stowed it inside his cloak.

Walter scratched his head. "Aren't you leaving evidence of where we're going?"

"None of your business. And this exercise is already extremely unorthodox, don't you think? Hop to it."

The Fox Thief scampered out the door. Walter and the others trailed after him. The smoke reduced the three guards in the hallway to their knees. Its thick clouds began to disperse.

Walter's adrenaline flew through his veins. "What are we looking for?"

"Stairs."

Guard shouts rang out from far behind the party. They rushed onward.

Tivara spoke up. "I hear echoes, like in a stairwell. Straight ahead."

The Fox Thief led the group to a pair of wood-and-silver doors. He whipped out his lockpicks and went to work on one.

Walter leaned over him. "Should I try to steal keys from the office?"

The Fox Thief bristled. "And spend our last free moments guessing which key is correct? No, thank you."

The latch clinked, and the Fox Thief pulled the door open. "After you, human. All you have to do is race to the top."

Walter set his hand on his hip. "That's not *all*, you know. There's unknown magic being carried around by someone we haven't laid eyes on yet."

Kylani sprinted past Walter through the open door. "For Pete's sake, Walter!"

He strode into the stairwell after her. Flickering torches lit the black stone space from high up its walls. Walter bounded up the stairs a short distance behind Kylani. Tivara and the Fox Thief ascended next.

With a cry of effort and annoyance, Gruhnt squeezed himself through the doorway.

Walter scoffed. "You'd think a prison would have bigger doors. Where do they house the ogres and orcs?"

The Fox Thief answered. "With the magma elves. In the dungeon. I've heard stories."

Walter's head spun at the diversity and expansiveness of Gladfire. "How many kinds of elves are there?"

"Twelve."

"I've met two."

"You'll meet more if you stay alive." The Fox Thief leapt up onto the step beside Walter and surpassed him. "Push yourself, human."

Walter clenched his jaws until his teeth shifted better into place. "I am."

The group stepped onto the last landing, graced with another set of silver-reinforced wooden doors.

Walter looked around. "This isn't right. Was that twenty stories?" He rushed to the single window and peered out between its metal bars. "There's no way we're high enough."

The Fox Thief stomped his foot. "We're in the shorter section of the tower."

Walter ran his hand through his hair and held the wavy locks back from his forehead. "What do we do?"

"We leave the stairwell through this door and find the way up to the spire."

Walter gestured to the doors. "There are probably guards out there."

"I know."

"How could this happen? How did we make a mistake like this? There's probably another set of stairs somewhere that goes all the way up from the first floor."

A tic of the Fox Thief's snout wrenched his whiskers to one side. "Watch your words, human. No thief, be it apprentice or master, wants to ever enter these black walls."

Walter remembered how much all five of them had at stake. He disliked the idea of leaving the stairway even more, and his guts tightened. "Everything could be lost if we go out that door and run into guards."

Tivara opened her mouth to speak.

The Fox Thief steadied her with gentle waves of his paw. His amber eyes never left Walter's. "Human, we have two main choices. Either we retrace our steps to the main floor and try to find an alternative stairway to the pinnacle, or you follow me through this door to whatever awaits us on the other side. The best option is, to me, quite obvious."

Walter gave a begrudging nod. "Now I understand why you wear that enchanted cloak all the time."

The Fox Thief grinned and pulled the hood closer around his face to better conceal himself.

One of the doors popped ajar, and Walter crept over to the crevice. He bumped into something he could barely see in the torch and day light. The Fox Thief ruffled his cloak and scoffed.

Walter cringed. "Sorry." He situated himself at the door's opening. Silence and a vacant hall greeted him. "It's clear."

Kylani muttered. "Says the human."

Tivara held her ear to the crack. "Walter's right. We should go."

A small fox paw appeared in the air, gesturing Walter forward. He led the rest of his group in following the thief down the corridor.

Walter's heart jumped at their good luck. Then fear swirled like smog in his chest, and his eyes darted all around them for someone lurking around a corner or a bookcase. "Any of you getting a creeping, funny feeling about this?"

The Fox Thief shushed him. "Enjoy good fortune until you have no reason to."

Soft footsteps dropped in an intersecting hallway coming up on Walter's right. The Fox Thief leapt up against the wall, pulling

Walter with him. Tivara, Kylani, and Gruhnt flattened themselves beside Walter as well as they could.

Walter lowered his volume to barely audible. "Do you have a weapon?"

The Fox Thief's paws emerged from his robe sleeves, practicing a few chops in the air.

Walter was about to inquire about any real, hand-held – or paw-held – weapons when the source of the footsteps walked into view. Human hands showed below silver bracers that matched the rest of a full set of dazzling armor. Walter stared at the clunky boots. How was such heavy equipment making such quiet sounds?

Walter leaned forward, intent on whispering a few more queries to the Fox Thief. Did they sneak past the guard? Did the thief throw another smoke bomb?

The Fox Thief's paw landed on Walter's chest and guided him back against the stone wall. "Patience."

Walter watched the guard. The man stood several inches over six feet tall. His shoulders must have made him an obvious pick for teams of various contact sports. Walter fidgeted. Being discovered by this fine figure of a brute did not fulfill any plans Walter had made for his life.

The guard moseyed in a half circle that brought him strolling back toward the party.

Walter lurched away from the wall. "We have to run. *Now.*"

The Fox Thief pointed to the guard. "Look."

Silver helmet, cuirass, bracers, and full leg armor. A massive, spiky mace swung from the guard's belt. His imposing stature housed what Walter assumed would prove to be an impressive amount of damage to deal to intruders such as themselves.

As the guard wandered closer, Walter squinted to examine the man further. His eyes, a cool shade of green, might as well have been closed for how little life shone in them. A dull, flat stare had replaced any healthy sheen and vibrancy they once held. Confidence and training didn't inform his plodding, slow gait. The man marched as if in a trance, on autopilot.

Walter chanced flourishing his hand in front of the guard's face. The guard remained transfixed on some point far beyond him. "It's like I'm wearing an enchanted cloak. But I'm not, right?" Ice-cold terror gripped Walter. "Are we too late? Did No free Mo and let him use necromancy on the guard? Tivara, what kind of magic is that?"

Tivara made a light trilling sound. "I'm not certain. It could be frost or nature magic. Perhaps we should keep thanking our lucky stars and move forward? Rrrow. It may merely be some of the magic Noraddian brought in with him in the corundum bars. He might've passed this way to reach Morattidus' cell."

The Fox Thief issued a decisive nod. "We should double our speed, then. Right. We're off."

The shadowy figure bolted down the corridor, and Walter jogged after him. A Repter guard in shimmering gold armor approached them at a snail's pace from another hallway. Drool trickled down from his sagging lower jaw. Walter and his companions raced past him. A tall, willowy moss elf protected by thick leather armor stumbled right at the group. They hurried around him.

The corridor opened up into a processing area replete with desks and metal shelves stuffed with books. The area's dead end brought the group to a halt, their only hope lying behind the double doors before them.

Walter consulted the books' spines. *Intake Names and Dates. Letters of the Law. Evidence and Sentencing. Releases.* "The stairs we're looking for have to be through those doors."

The Fox Thief motioned Walter ahead. "Why don't you open one? You have the most reservations about taking new avenues."

Walter tugged on a door handle. "It's locked. Your expertise is required yet again."

The Fox Thief scurried to the door and adjusted his small metal tools in the lock.

When the click of victory arrived within seconds, Walter marveled at the thief's skill. "Will you teach me to do that one day?"

The Fox Thief chuckled as he secured his lockpicks and eased the door open. "Don't press your luck too much, human."

"No, I'm serious. It's a skill I might need someday, and you're the best teacher around."

"I'm not a teacher. I put the skill to use for myself and my personal gain." The Fox Thief pattered up the first few steps of the newly accessed stairwell.

"What would it take for you to change your mind and mentor me?" Walter tried to sprint up the stairs beside the Fox Thief, but his severely taxed stamina left him tripping over his own feet.

The Fox Thief chattered in unintelligible sounds before he answered. "I'll make a deal with you. If you study with no fewer than six teachers and perform for me a priceless service, I will *consider* allowing you to apprentice with me."

Walter's eyebrows skyrocketed. "That's a deal. Officially. We have three witnesses."

Kylani groaned, running up the stairs past Walter. "Don't encourage him, thief. He dabbles in practically every single skill we can learn in Gladfire."

The Fox Thief's eyes widened in panic. "Get down!" He flung himself prostrate on the stair.

Walter dove out of the way, slamming into Kylani. They fell hard on the black stone steps. Tivara and Gruhnt hung back against the opposite wall.

The Fox Thief trembled and picked himself up. He inspected something on the stair above him. Walter brushed his stinging palm against his leather cuirass and leaned in at the Fox Thief's side.

The Vulyon pointed a claw at a narrow beige thread. "There." He lifted it with his paw. "False alarm. I'm sorry. This tripwire has already been severed. I prefer to be overly cautious when I see the hints of traps."

Walter glanced at the walls. "What does the thread go to? What does it trigger?"

"Duck down again."

Walter and his other companions sank low on their haunches. The Fox Thief jumped two stairs down and yanked on the thread. A net of thick ropes dropped from the ceiling. Black volcanic rocks weighted it. As it crashed onto the stairs, the rocks snapped together beneath it.

The Fox Thief discarded the thread. "Magnets and, most likely, magic. We would've been trapped here for sure until the guards came."

Walter picked himself up. "Are we guessing there's only one creature who would've disarmed that trap and is headed up to free Morattidus right now?"

"It's about time you treated this with the seriousness it deserves. Yes. No more stops until we've accomplished what we entered to do. To the top!"

All five companions urged themselves up the stairwell against the aching, screaming fibers of their exhausted muscles. They heaved stiff boots upward and forced their lungs to extract another bellyful of air. Walter's legs threatened to tear and give out, but he let the contents of the recent newspaper articles fill his mind. Necromancy and dead Rodae and mourning villages and a rich brother-in-law with enchanted corundum trumped sore sinews today.

They almost collapsed on the top landing, identical to the one on the tenth floor. Walter wasted no time peering through the barred window at the sky level with them and the landscape below. The Fox Thief whipped one of the double doors open, and Walter stayed close on his heels.

After the cramped stairwell and maze of corridors, this room gaped wide and long. The ceiling yawned high above them. Three cells occupied each of the walls on their left, right, and straight ahead. The fifteen-foot cages' thinly spaced silver bars glowed white-blue with swirling, shifting magic.

Several ingots of red-, blue-, and yellow-specked corundum lay in a haphazard line on the floor leading away from the room's only entrance. They pointed Walter's attention to the room's center.

A five-foot-tall Rodae covered in light grey-brown fur fast advanced on a guard manning the single desk. Draped in a green silk tunic with metallic gold trim and baggy brown velvet pants, the Rodae could've been any one of the city residents Walter had shared the Crimson Jewel's streets with.

The guard rose to his substantial height, towering over the Rodae. "You're not employed here. How did you get in this room?"

The Rodae reached into his olive-green satin satchel and pulled out a block of corundum. He aimed it at the guard and squealed. Vines shot up out of the floor, splitting cracks between the stones. The vines grew in rapid tendrils that encased the guard's legs and arms. The Rodae let the spent corundum bar clatter to the floor as the vines jerked the guard into his chair and constricted him there. He shouted, and a vine snaked its way across his mouth, muffling his cries.

The Rodae took off for the nearest cell on Walter's left. A short figure sat crumpled against the back wall. The approaching rat-man squeaked in rushed, high-pitched tones. "Can you hear me? What did they do to you?"

Walter reset his tense fingers around the handle of his speedy hunting knife. "Noraddian!"

The well-dressed Rodae turned. His brown eyes enlarged into perfect circles. One pink paw flew to a golden emerald amulet around his neck. The other paw shot into his satchel.

Tivara raised her paws. Fireballs appeared in front of them. "Careful, Walter. His jewelry could be enchanted with anything."

Walter nodded. "We want to talk to you, Noraddian. In peace. We're just scared of what kind of magic you hold in the corundum you bought."

Kylani whispered. "It's plainly nature magic, Walt."

Walter cleared his throat a few times. "Okay, we know you're using nature magic to break into this prison and break your brother-in-law out. We're sorry for the loss of your sister."

Noraddian released a torrent of squeaks. "It was a travesty what happened to her." He approached the cell's door and extracted a block of corundum from his satchel.

"Whoa!" Walter advanced a few steps toward him. "We can't let you help Morattidus escape. He's a dangerous creature."

Noraddian narrowed his eyes at Walter, baring his long teeth. "The duke and his selfishness – his laziness – his downright stupidity are the dangers we should all fight against. We pleaded with him so many times to protect our village. He wouldn't. It would've cost him so little. Instead, we paid prices too high to bear." Noraddian extended the corundum bar at the cell door.

"No!" Walter strode another six feet forward. He held his knife up. "Noraddian, seriously, put the corundum down and walk away from that door. We don't want to hurt you. We know your heart is hurting, and you're trying to do what you think is right."

"Where did you get your information from? The newspapers and the flyers they post up around town?" Noraddian directed the corundum at Walter. "Nobody told you how many of the duke's guards he could suddenly spare to tackle my brother-in-law to the ground. Nobody reported anywhere that he wept uncontrollably for his deceased wife as they carted him into one of their cells on wheels."

Walter inched back. He thought he saw the shadowy form of the Fox Thief steal away from the rest of the group and travel in a wide, silent circle toward Noraddian's blind spot. "Take it easy, sir. No, those parts of the story weren't in any of the pages we read. And we certainly weren't sent by the duke. But we've climbed twenty stories' worth of stairs the same as you. We're here now, and our skills are strong. Maybe we can assist you."

Noraddian snorted. "Oh, you're the one who shows up too late to give any real aid and thinks an offer of condolences will solve the problem. Well, you are too late, and whatever powers you have, you don't have a pouch full of enchanted corundum. I suggest you take your half-baked schemes and climb your way down from this tower."

"Not gonna happen." Walter pointed his knife at the shadow behind Noraddian. "Get him!"

Nothing changed. No one attacked Noraddian or snatched the corundum out of his paw. No one cut the vines surrounding the guard at his desk. The ensuing silence and stillness made Walter wish like hell he could've sneezed or even farted to break it up.

He located a petite shadow lingering behind him near the open door. "Fox Thief? Is that you? I thought you went around past Noraddian."

The Fox Thief huffed. "This is your fight, human. I'm merely your guide."

"Dang it." Walter moved toward Noraddian. Hearing Gruhnt's armor shift as he joined Walter kept the young human's knees from buckling. "Noraddian, I'll ask you one more time. Get away from that door. Do *not* release its prisoner. Let's work something out and take care of your village before any more creatures get killed."

"You don't listen, do you? I didn't empty my bank accounts to give up this close to my brother-in-law and shit on my sister's memory."

Noraddian jerked the block of corundum toward Walter. Yellow dust flew in a circling swarm at his face and tickled his nostrils. He sneezed so hard, he bent over in half and almost collapsed to the floor.

Tivara explained the attack in a stern word. "Pollen. Kylani, shoot to wound. Gruhnt, try to grab his satchel."

Kylani set an arrow to her bowstring. Gruhnt charged at Noraddian. The ogre-orc raised his mace high and swung it down at the Rodae's green satchel.

Noraddian scampered backwards and dropped the depleted corundum. He grabbed another enchanted brick from his bag. He thrust it at Gruhnt. Grey particles flew out of it, encasing Gruhnt's spiked mace in bulky stone. Its increased weight pulled Gruhnt's arm down in a fast, uncontrolled arc that extended the weapon out behind him.

Walter's eyes watered, dropping tears on the floor. He wiped at them with his sleeves. "Tivara, what's going on? I can't see."

Kylani's voice answered him. "I'm about to peg the rat."

She let her arrow go, hoping to pin Noraddian's shirt between the cell bars. Her arrow soared at his shoulder.

Noraddian discarded his used corundum. He pivoted and held his satchel up as a shield. Kylani's arrow pierced the satin and dinged off a bar of corundum. Noraddian pulled the arrow free and tossed it away.

Walter dried his eyes in time to watch Tivara stream long ribbons of fire at Noraddian. Their flicking tips ended a few feet from him.

Tivara's eyes took on a strange look, like they were both infinite and shallow. Their own golden hue disappeared, taken over by the yellow-tinged orange of her flames. "Surrender, rat. Or I might forget my civility and roast you for my supper. Rrrow."

Kylani reloaded her bow. Noraddian procured two magic-wrapped corundum blocks. One of them percussed the air with a succession of wet clay splatters. The first clay burst stuck to Kylani's arrow point, rendering it overburdened and soft. The second spray of clay slapped Kylani square in the face, knocking her back a few paces. The final clay burst knocked the short bow out of her hand.

Tivara edged toward Noraddian, extending her flame ribbons closer to his satchel. Noraddian hid behind the other enchanted corundum bar. It erected a wall of sand between himself and Tivara's fire.

The flames penetrated the sand, making it glow a dazzling bright yellow. Tivara gasped and cut off her magic. The sand compacted, glowing red before it cooled into a foot-thick wall of glass the same height as Noraddian.

The Rodae traded his spent corundum for a new bar from his bag.

Walter ran at him. "I got this, Tivara."

Walter dove in, plotting to cut the satchel's strap with his hunting knife in the blink of an eye. Noraddian barely positioned the pulsing corundum block between them before Walter could slice the satin strap. A gust of wind slammed into Walter's chest. The air rushed out of his lungs, and he landed on the floor. The force of both impacts left him sore, shocked, and moaning.

Noraddian threw the normal corundum behind him. "I warned you."

Gruhnt beat his stone-encapsulated mace against the floor until the last of the rock broke away from its iron spikes. He twisted his mouth into a wide, grinning grimace.

Walter panted for breath and took heart. "So... did... we."

Gruhnt thundered around the glass wall and whirled the mace at Noraddian's arm. He connected with the Rodae, sending him hurtling through the air. Noraddian crashed into the side of Morattidus' cell and crumpled to the floor. Gruhnt closed in on Noraddian while the much-smaller Rodae cowered, rubbing his injured arm.

Walter coached himself into rolling on his side and pushing himself up to sitting. Kylani slung her clay-covered arrow away with a sharp cry of aggravation and wiped wet clay off her bow. Tivara moved closer to Walter, maneuvering herself past the glass wall for another straight shot at Noraddian.

Gruhnt extended his empty hand to the Rodae. "Will you hand over your corundum, please?"

Noraddian executed a forward roll between Gruhnt's legs. He popped up behind the ogre-orc and brandished a sparkling corundum brick.

Tivara exploded twin flames into existence. "Gruhnt, look out!" She shoved the fireballs at Noraddian, burning two matching holes into the back of his silk shirt.

Noraddian emitted an ear-splitting squeak. The corundum bar fumbled from his paw.

Gruhnt grabbed the satin satchel and ripped it off Noraddian's shoulder.

The Rodae snarled and wrapped his pink paw around his emerald pendant. "I believe you have something of mine and you want to return it."

Gruhnt's green cheeks blazed pink. "I'm sorry." He hung the satchel over Noraddian's shoulder and gave it a gentle pat.

Walter wobbled as he rose to his feet. "You gotta be kidding me."

Tivara spared him a quick glance. "Charisma enchantment. We have to finish this fight, or he'll talk us out of our weapons next."

Noraddian jerked two corundum ingots from his satchel. "No more talk."

Quicksand sprang up under Kylani's boots. The animate sand slurped at her legs, dragging her down to her hands and knees. She shrieked and kicked, but it engulfed her calves and forearms. It blanketed her short bow.

The other piece of corundum veered toward Walter. He leapt out of the way as a torrent of ocean-blue water gushed at high velocity toward where he'd stood.

Walter hadn't gotten this near to the vine-trapped guard yet. His weary eyes roamed the guard, who struggled in the tiny wriggles his confines allowed him. Walter rifled his hair with a new conundrum. Did he cut the guard free to battle beside him and his compatriots?

Tivara's shout jerked him back to his group. "Walter!"

The human's spine snapped up straight, and his blood surged fast despite the chill that congealed it. Gruhnt curved his mace at Noraddian's chest. Tivara fired a dozen bite-sized flames at Noraddian.

The Rodae grabbed hold of Gruhnt's mace, and its momentum flung him toward the ceiling. Tivara's flames landed on the vacant floor. Noraddian curled his paws around one of the cell's silver bars and slid down beside the cage door. He snatched a piece of enchanted corundum from his satchel in each paw.

Walter reeled in disbelief. "Did you have to buy twenty-five of those?"

Noraddian issued a thick white mist at Tivara that enveloped her. She tried to ignite her fire magic, but the suspended water droplets dowsed each attempt with a hissing sizzle.

The Rodae's other enchanted block grew a wall of thorns around Gruhnt. The ogre-orc cracked his mace against it and yelped in pain as prickly points shifted to gouge his cheek. Red blood with a green shine glistened on Gruhnt's skin and the offending thorns.

His friends' torment and sacrifice braced Walter's nerves. His exhaustion and how much he wanted to crawl into a bed for a ten-hour sleep crept to the back of his mind. He stalked toward Noraddian, scowling. "I don't care how high your level is compared to mine. Nobody hurts my friends without me doing something about it."

Noraddian peeked inside his satchel. His eyes widened in alarm as Walter reached him.

"All out of magic?" Walter slashed his hunting knife at the satchel's strap.

The blade sliced the satin clean through, and the satchel fell to the floor.

Noraddian puffed up his chest, and the emerald glinted in his golden necklace.

Walter squinted with clear intent. "Nuh-uh. No more talking." He arced the knife out toward Noraddian, nicking the side of the Rodae's neck. A drop of blood stained his fur.

Noraddian snatched up the satchel by its broken strap and slung it at Walter's legs. What Walter expected to be a soft thwap of fabric collided against his calf with a hard, broad surface. Walter's arms sprawled as he careened toward the floor. He landed with an exhale, making sure he kept hold of his knife.

Refusing to stay down, Walter dragged himself to his feet. "You're saving some magic for later?"

Noraddian swung the satchel at Walter's middle.

Walter sucked his stomach in and jumped back. "You're not knocking me down again, and I'm not letting you put the rest of that magic to use."

Kylani shouted from the mess of quicksand continuing to suck her toward the floor. "Go for his neck, Walter! You already damaged him there."

Tivara sounded distant from her misty enclosure. "Remember your healing potion if you get into trouble."

Gruhnt broke a few thorns off his living cage with his mace. New ones grew in their place.

Noraddian slashed at Walter's arm with his short, white claws. Walter ducked aside and poked Noraddian's neck wound with his knife's tip.

Kylani grunted with the effort of fighting the quicksand's hold. "Use the bag against him, Walt! He thinks it's protecting him, or he wouldn't try to carry it now."

Gruhnt managed to take his shield off his back. He bashed it against the wall of thorns. "A bag isn't a shield."

Walter nodded, his understanding of Gruhnt's point taking root in his bones. "Just like a stick isn't a real sword."

Walter jabbed his knife through the top of the satchel and drove it down through the satin panels. His blade clanged against corundum, and two ingots slid out of the rent bag.

Noraddian exposed his teeth and flung the ruined satchel against the cell bars. He lunged at Walter, scratching the human's elbows through his woolen tunic sleeves.

Walter scrunched his eyebrows low. "Hey, one of my neighbors spun this shirt for me." He counterattacked, stabbing Noraddian's arm through his silk shirt.

Noraddian's eyes flashed wild. His claws scraped Walter's cheek. He sank his sharp teeth into Walter's neck where his leather cuirass failed to protect him.

Walter screamed and redoubled his efforts to wrangle Noraddian into cooperation. Walter pushed Noraddian away as hard as he could.

Tivara howled. "The potion, Walter!"

Walter plucked the green vial from his pocket. Noraddian knocked it out of his hand, and it rolled across the floor. Walter scrambled after the potion. Noraddian kicked Walter in his side's tender flesh with more voracity than Walter expected from a short rat-man. Soreness welled up in Walter's body as he wrapped his hand around the bottle's neck.

Noraddian punted the bottle out of Walter's grasp across the room. He swatted Walter's hands down and leaned, snarling, into Walter's face. Clawed pink paws squeezed around Walter's neck. Noraddian seethed inches from Walter's nose. "Silly human. Did you think I was born in that posh Golden Silks penthouse? I come from the same village my sister died in. And this is how we fought for our food and our lives. Not with beguiling words, but with our claws and teeth." Noraddian pushed on Walter's windpipe, restricting his airflow almost to nothing.

Walter made sickly whistling sounds trying to draw what oxygen he could into his tired lungs. *No, not tired. We must fight!* Walter dug his hunting knife into Noraddian's belly up to its iron hilt.

Noraddian's spreading grin shook with pain. "You can't best me. I've been scrapping since long before your mother met your father, let alone bore you."

"You don't know my parents!" Walter retracted the hunting knife.

Noraddian grabbed Walter's head and smacked the back of it against the rigid stone floor. "I don't want to!"

Pure agony stabbed through Walter's skull. He punctured Noraddian's belly a second time.

Sweet relief flooded Walter from his head – which didn't ache so much anymore – to the tips of his blistered toes.

Noraddian sneered at him. "The magic I paid for will keep your friends from saving your life until long after I'm gone with my brother-in-law."

Walter relaxed against the unforgiving floor, enjoying every languid breath. "It seems like you want me to congratulate you."

"You might as well. Why not?"

"Because you forgot something. Two things, actually. You should congratulate me."

Noraddian's eyelids twinged.

Walter picked his head up off the floor and stared straight into Noraddian's eyes. "I leveled up, and not only should you say *grats* to me as a good sportsman, but that makes me feel like a whole new man."

Walter pulled his knife blade out of Noraddian's belly and stove it into the Rodae's bleeding neck wound.

Noraddian leapt back, keeping the knife from penetrating very deeply.

Walter sprang to his feet.

Tivara, Gruhnt, and Kylani erupted in cheers.

The sky elf formed a shrill, loud whistle. "Get him, Walter!"

Walter charged at Noraddian. The Rodae flattened himself against the floor, dodging Walter's blade strikes. Noraddian's teeth pierced Walter's ankle through his leather greaves. Walter cried out and kicked Noraddian away.

Noraddian vaulted into the air, pummeling Walter to the floor. "It won't work, human. You're no match for me. No matter how many levels you gain today."

He stomped on Walter's right wrist until Walter's fingers released their grip on the knife's handle. Noraddian's foot sent the weapon sliding across the floor, where it banged against the front of the guard's desk.

Noraddian kicked the underside of Walter's chin, making his teeth clatter together. "Stay out of my way, and you get to keep your life."

Noraddian deposited a firm heel stomp into Walter's stomach. The Rodae rushed to the two twinkling corundum bars and scooped them up. He aimed one at the cell door, and a seed's green tendril snaked its way out of the lock. The stem grew and hardened into a sapling's brown-bark trunk. The lock's mechanisms snapped, and the door swung ajar.

"Morattidus! Are you all right?" Noraddian scampered into the cell and shoved his shoulder up under his brother-in-law's arm to support him. "What kind of spell do they have you under?"

Walter rolled his head to one side and peeked into the cell. Morattidus teetered on his feet. A white streak graced his charcoal-grey fur, running down from the top of his head and tapering off past his left eye. A ragged, dirty burlap tunic hung to Morattidus' knees. Its tattered V-neck opening showed his white chest. He stood mere inches taller than his brother-in-law.

Morattidus attempted to smile, but the effect was weak. His black eyes trailed in restless patterns over the floor. "Strong magic. You timed your arrival well. They haven't struck me with it since this morning."

"I have one enchanted piece of corundum left. I can save it for our escape, or I can wake you up."

Morattidus' eyes flashed, and the corners of his mouth perked up. "Help me, brother. Once I'm fully roused, we'll have no need for any more magic rocks."

Tivara screeched through her watery prison. "Stop him, Walter!"

Walter got halfway to his feet, looking for the exact position of his hunting knife. The strong echoes of laughter stopped him and called his attention back to Morattidus' cell.

Golden beams of sunlight streamed from Noraddian's final corundum bar. They bathed Morattidus, who unfurled into a proud, regal posture. His eyes, no longer aimless, glinted with pointed malice.

Morattidus pointed a claw at Walter.

Walter's feet and lower legs numbed and tingled. Unable to feel them, he toppled over. He rubbed at them with vigorous strokes through his leather greaves. Horror seized him that his nerves and muscles might be permanently dead.

Boot steps grew louder in the stairwell outside the room's open door. Harsh voices, men's and women's, bounced off the walls in a startling cacophony.

Morattidus didn't bat an eyelid. He strolled out of his cell as the first guards marched in. Morattidus lifted his claw at the vanguard, a tall, chiseled specimen who appeared half-human, half-moss elf. The guard's orders cut off, his mouth gaping. His earth-colored skin drained to grey. Cracks split in his cheeks as they dried and caved in. He collapsed on the floor.

The other guards fanned out, waving their swords and maces at Morattidus. One guard, a broad-shouldered ogress in silver armor, advanced ahead of the rest. Morattidus cupped his paws together in front of him. The ogress froze in place. Her wide neck constricted and flaked skin onto her armor's detailed contours. Morattidus stepped up to her and drew a long, steady breath.

Two additional guards flanked him, and he spared them the briefest of glances. His inhale finished, Morattidus sprayed bright-green mist into the guards' faces. They wailed and screeched. They tried to pry their helmets off but dropped motionless to the floor.

Walter's eyes felt large and round enough to tumble out of his head. Another half dozen guards poured into the room.

Kylani yelped in surprise. The quicksand dried up around her arms and legs. It disappeared, and she gathered up her bow and arrow.

Walter looked for the glass wall, but it had faded as well. The guard who had spent a solid half hour trapped in his desk chair sprinted at Morattidus.

Walter called after him. "No!"

Tivara's mist dissipated, and she shook water droplets off her cloak. Gruhnt's capsule of thorns crumbled into nothing.

Tivara's eyes met Walter's. "There's nothing we can do. We have to get out of the prison."

Walter nodded and made a beeline for the open door to the stairwell. A small but sturdy force stopped him, propped against his stomach.

The Fox Thief's furry red-and-white face appeared from the shadows of his enchanted cloak. "I scoped out a better exit for us while you were fighting."

Walter smirked although he appreciated the Vulyon's expertise. "It's good of you to do *something*."

"I also fulfilled your promise to me." The Fox Thief opened one side of his magic cloak. Several pockets bulged with corundum bars. "This way."

Walter jogged after the Fox Thief to a wooden hatch painted the same black as the stone floor around it. The Vulyon ripped the hatch open, exposing a long ladder beneath its square hole.

Walter fidgeted. Another wave of guards rolled in from the stairwell. Morattidus greeted them with maniacal chuckles and spewed black spittle into their faces. Noraddian cowered in the open cell, covering his eyes.

Tivara patted Walter stiffly on the arm. "I know what we came to do, but we're severely outranked. We did all we could."

Walter watched guard after guard – Cantia, Fee'li, orc, human – succumb to Morattidus' unfathomable magic. "All those people and creatures out there in Gladfire – they'll be vulnerable to this. Most of them are probably unarmed and don't know how to fight. Look at how he's destroying those guards."

The Fox Thief bounced down through the hole and caught hold of the ladder. "I'm not sticking around for whatever you have in mind. I'm getting out, and you can either join me or wind up like the guards. That's up to you."

"I only need time for one thing." Walter bolted around the guard's desk and retrieved Slithe's hunting knife from the floor. He returned to the hatch in time to follow Gruhnt down the ladder. Walter reached up and drew the hatch closed over them.

Sparse light emanated from far-spaced torches embedded into the wall behind the climbing party. They said nothing, each harboring their own thoughts and repeating the motion of one foot after the other for a seeming eternity.

Walter felt the difference of planting his boot soles on gritty stone rather than a narrow wood slat. He reveled in a breath of gratitude before stealing after his comrades through a door in the narrow chamber. They careened down an empty hallway and flew out the door at its end.

The orange and pink of twilight blazed in the sky over the prison's outer wall. Gruhnt took up a post against the wall and hoisted each of the others over the top. He pulled himself up and dropped with a shuddering collision of boots against ground beside the rest of the group.

Kylani held her palm up to Tivara. "I'd like to be paid for my services."

Walter's head dropped to one side. "You're not traveling with us anymore? Not even to get out of the Chokehold?"

"No. I need to disappear. I already had the Isolated Six hunting me down. I don't need a crazy, powerful necromancer spotting me with all of you."

Tivara counted out silver coins into Kylani's palm. "Thank you for your help, anyway."

Walter laid a hand on Kylani's arm. "We made a good team. I'm not ready to say goodbye."

The Fox Thief reached his paws up to Tivara. "I'd appreciate the rest of my compensation, too, before I split my own way."

Walter gave the Fox Thief some of his own coins in addition to Tivara's. "Thanks for leading us safely in and out."

"No problem. Thank you for hiring the best thief in the world."

"You were mighty impressive. I'll admit that much. But we're still debating if you're the absolute best or not."

Kylani slipped a few paces away.

Walter pursued her. "We can't convince you to stick with us, even a few hours longer?"

"A snowball stands a bigger chance in front of an angry fire mage." Kylani paused her hasty exit. "You don't need me, Walt."

"Will I – or we – ever see you again?" A lump caught low in Walter's throat.

Kylani faked an upbeat tone that fell flat. "Maybe."

"But you doubt it."

Kylani shrugged. "You keep adventuring, and I keep traveling. There are a lot of fields and woods and cities and towns in Gladfire. And I gotta go." Kylani gave a short hum of remembrance and lifted a handful of red clay from her pocket. "This is yours."

"Keep it. I don't know any recipes for red clay yet."

"You will." Kylani pulled Walter's pocket open and dropped the clay in. "Oh, and grats. You deserve it." Kylani patted Walter's shoulder and darted off through a gap between thick tree trunks into the forest.

Gruhnt lifted his hand and waved.

Walter looked for the Fox Thief's hazy shadow to take his aching heart off Kylani. "Anyway, fox, we–"

Tivara pointed to another part of the forest. Leaves and thin branches shuddered, moving deeper into the foliage. Soon, the visible trees rested still.

Walter draped his hand over the back of his neck. "He left without saying goodbye?"

"It'll be all right, Walter." Tivara adjusted the drape of her hood over her ears. "We should squeeze our way out of the Chokehold as well."

Walter's eyes watered as he gazed at the prison's outer wall. He sensed he was facing the place where Slithe died and might continue to lean against the wagon. Walter couldn't be sure.

"We don't want to get captured."

Tivara and Gruhnt snuck toward the forest.

A tear rolled down Walter's cheek. "I can't."

They spun to gawk at him.

"How can I?" Walter gestured to the wall and all it hid behind it. "I almost died. Slithe bled out, and lots of guards were decayed to death by a necromancer. Kylani's gone, and the Fox Thief who rescued us – twice – abandoned us."

Tivara ran back and grabbed Walter's wrist. "Come on. I'm prepared to make a deal with you, if you want. Leave with us now, and I'll owe you a favor, whatever you choose."

A spot of warmth glowed in Walter's fractured heart. "Anything?"

Chapter 11

The red-and-white-gingham blankets stretched out over half of the Grass family's yard. Walter's youngest siblings chirruped and gasped at Gruhnt's massive size. They climbed up one side of the seated ogre-orc and tumbled off his shoulders in every direction. He giggled and helped them up off the ground.

Hovan beamed at Walter and reached over to ruffle his hair. "I'm busting with pride in you, boy. I sent you out with an old sword. You came back with an enchanted blade and two kinds of armor on."

Marabee interrupted her conversation with Tivara to send a sidelong frown to Hovan. "I know exactly how you sent my son out into the world, Dad. We haven't forgotten."

Walter cleared his throat and held his hands out to attract his friends' attention. Tivara and Gruhnt looked at him. "I've been meaning to address this whole multiple armors thing. After seeing Slithe and the Fox Thief – and both of you and Kylani – in action, I've decided to quit thinking that being a Jack of all skills is a smart approach to adventuring."

Tivara applauded. "Slithe would've loved to hear you say that."

Gruhnt smiled as another of Walter's brothers rolled down his back. "That's a lovely compliment, Walter. I'm happy you'll be joining us in honing your skills."

Walter tugged on his leather cuirass. "I'm not sure medium armor is right for me. I was glad for the protection of it when Noraddian bit me–"

Marabee stared at Walter, pale with terror.

Walter held up his thumb and index finger spaced a quarter inch apart. "It was a tiny bite, Mom. My greave absorbed most of the damage."

Marabee swatted Hovan's knee with a sharp but glancing smack.

Redley winked at his son.

Walter grinned and refocused on Tivara and Gruhnt. "Anyway, I really admired Noraddian's ability to move around so easily. I don't think I want to try cloth armor like Tivara, but I'd be interested in trading my medium leather for some light leather."

Marabee picked up some of the empty plates and bowls from the blanket. "Children, time to clean up. Stop treating our guest like a ladder and slide."

The older half of Walter's siblings fell into line. Seated quietly in the spaces between Walter, his elders, and his friends, they stacked their bowls into a tower. One sister carried them away, and the other oldest siblings carted off serving platters scattered with crumbs.

Gruhnt raised his index finger. One of the sisters paused with her platter at Gruhnt's side. He angled the platter, scooping the remaining morsels into his mouth.

Marabee chuckled. "Thank you, Gruhnt. I'm pleased you like our humble cuisine."

Walter sat up straighter. "Actually, Mum, we had lunch with Gruhnt's family once. Their food isn't all that different. They just have more game meat and wild vegetables."

Gruhnt stuck his tongue out, stained cobalt blue. "My mother never made blue-mushroom ravioli."

Walter pointed at him. "I told you, right?" Walter slid his tongue out as far as he could.

Marabee shook her head and stood up. "Redley. Dad. We should give our guests of honor some time to talk alone. They've had a rough journey."

Hovan's azure eyes twinkled. "I believe it's called a quest."

Walter responded with a deep nod. Satisfaction belied the solemn purse of his lips.

Redley supported Hovan in getting up from the checkered blanket. The young children scattered, some running into the house ahead of Marabee. Others raced each other toward the well.

Walter picked at a grass blade standing by the blanket's edge. The silence that graced the yard felt good and restorative after the mission, the escape from the Chokehold's heavy vegetation, and the intense welcome he received at home. "I'm serious about selecting the skills I want to work on. I know my previous approach worried you both."

Tivara set her mouth in a line. "That's fine, Walter. It's not your skill set that worries me."

"Noraddian and Morattidus?" Walter guessed.

Gruhnt chimed in. "No and Mo."

Tivara met Gruhnt's humor with a serious tone. "We don't know what else they did at the prison or where they went afterward. We have no idea of their grander plan."

Walter retrieved Slithe's black ribbon charm bracelet from his pocket. "There's Slithe's dying intention, too. What do we do about the rest of the Isolated Six and their prisoners?"

Tivara shook her head. "I don't know. As much as I'd love to help them, I believe Morattidus' threat takes priority."

Walter's heart sped up for a few beats. "Priority for what? Forming another party? Accepting another quest?"

Tivara folded one paw over the other in her lap. "I think so. Mrow. We succeeded in what we originally set out to do. We transported the invisibility potions to the Crimson Jewel."

"And eventually met up with Noraddian."

"You leveled up three times. What level does that make you now?"

Walter gleamed. "Six."

Tivara gave a start. "You were level three when I took you out of Hustle Hub? Brrow, I'm glad I didn't know how green you were."

Gruhnt laughed. "You were such a noob, Walter."

Walter pouted. "I was not."

Gruhnt rested his hand over his spasming belly. "You barely had any armor when we found you."

"So what? It worked, and it was brand new."

Tivara curled up on her side on the gingham blanket. "That armor did save your life."

Walter plucked the blade of grass and tied it into a knot. "It did. I'm glad I was able to grab Slithe's knife before we fled the prison. I'm mad I lost the healing potion you gave me, though."

"We'll get more."

"When?" Walter threw the knotted grass beyond the blanket. "There's a high-level necromancer melting people's faces. His brother-in-law has wicked charisma and unarmed fighting skills. I still don't have a ton of money, and our party has been reduced to the three of us. That is, if we even *are* a party anymore. Maybe you two just brought me home to make sure I didn't die from some enraged killer-bee swarm. Maybe you just wanted to sample my mom's cooking."

Tivara lifted her head. "Walter. Mrow."

Walter dared to meet Tivara's gaze. "What?"

Her expression softened. "I don't have to ask Gruhnt's opinion to know we're both still in this with you. The original mission – quest – was given to me by a friend. I'm still going to question him and try to find out where Morattidus is."

Walter fiddled with his bootlaces. "Even though you were only tasked with delivering two bottles to Noraddian, you're going to accept the larger quest and search for answers?"

"Of course. When I worked in the hospital, I pledged to heal the sick and wounded creatures who requested our aid. I don't live my life much differently in general rrow. If we don't investigate, who will? And with Morattidus and Noraddian on the loose, there could be a lot more creatures made sick and hurt."

Walter crawled toward Tivara across the blankets. He held his hand out palm down in the middle of their circle. "If you're heading out into the dangers of Gladfire, I'm going with you."

Tivara placed her paw over Walter's hand. "We'll put a proper party together, Walter. You'll see. Hrow."

Gruhnt stacked his giant green hand on top of Tivara's paw. "Count me in."

Walter wondered at his friends. "When do we leave?"

"We can take a few days to rest."

Walter raised an eyebrow. "Stop by Hustle Hub to pick up supplies?"

Gruhnt stretched his wide mouth into a dreamy but menacing grimace. "I can trade in my iron mace for a bronze one."

Walter laid his other hand over Gruhnt's. "I know I might die. I might run out of money completely – again – and embarrass myself in countless ways. I know it means leaving my family again, but I can't wait."

About the Author

Photo © 2017 Joshua Leuthold

Cassandra Leuthold started writing at age seven and never really stopped. She loves combining what most people think of as opposites: the magical and the everyday, the modern and the vintage, the darkest nights and the brightest joys.

Even while she's delving deep into fictional worlds, she remains a tea aficionado, DIY crafter, and unapologetic music junkie.

Cassandra stretches out with her writer husband and their tuxedo lap cat, Gaia, in a house three sizes too big. She holds a Bachelor's in Liberal Studies and a Master's in English.

Get a reader's guidebook to amazing fiction and unlock VIP website access for free at www.cassandraleuthold.com/vip.

www.ingramcontent.com/pod-product-compliance
Lightning Source LLC
Chambersburg PA
CBHW030226180626
46810CB00008B/2982